KENTUCKY DREAMER

GOLDEN FILLY SERIES

KENTUCKY DREAMER

LAURAINE SNELLING

BETHANY HOUSE PUBLISHERS
MINNEAPOLIS, MINNESOTA 55438

Cover illustration by Brett Longley,
Bethany House Publishers staff artist.

Published by Bethany House Publishers
A Ministry of Bethany Fellowship, Inc.
6820 Auto Club Road, Minneapolis, Minnesota 55438

Printed in the United States of America

Library of Congress Cataloging-in-Publication Data

Snelling, Lauraine.
    Kentucky Dreamer / Lauraine Snelling.
       p. cm. — (Golden filly series ; bk. 4)
    Summary: Having won the Santa Anita Derby, Trish and her horse
look forward to competing in the Kentucky Derby, until a series of
misfortunes interferes with their dream.

    [1. Horse racing—Fiction. 2. Family problems—Fiction.
3. Christian life—Fiction.] I. Title.
II. Series: Snelling, Lauraine. Golden filly series ; bk. 4.
PZ7.S677Ke   1992
[Fic]—dc20   91-42639
                                                        CIP
ISBN 1–55661–234–6   AC

To Wayne,
whose love and support
make it possible for me to fly.

LAURAINE SNELLING is a full-time writer who has authored several published books, sold articles for a wide range of magazines, and written weekly features in local newspapers. She also teaches writing courses and trains people in speaking skills. She and her husband, Wayne, have two grown children and make their home in California.

Her lifelong love of horses began at age five with a pony named Polly and continued with Silver, Kit, Rowdy, and her daughter's horse Cimeron, which starred in her first children's book *Tragedy on the Toutle*.

CHAPTER 1

They must have talked half the night.

Tricia Evanston stretched and yawned. It felt as if she had just fallen asleep, but she knew that since the birds were already singing, her thoroughbred horse, Spitfire, winner of yesterday's Santa Anita Derby, would be wanting his breakfast. She tossed a pillow on the body sleeping in the other bed.

"Go 'way." Her best friend since kindergarten, Rhonda Seaboldt, knocked the pillow to the floor.

"Well, if you'd rather stay in bed—but I need to eat breakfast and get to the track. If you're coming, you'd better hustle." Trish hit the floor running. "Dad said he'd meet us in the lobby at 7:00," she called from the bathroom.

Trish stared at her image in the mirror. *Wow! Winning jockey of the Santa Anita Derby!* How come her face didn't look any different? She finger-combed her dark, wavy hair up off her face. Shouldn't you look, well, more grown up than sixteen when you and the true-black horse you've raised from a colt has just won the Santa Anita Derby? When you've met and defeated world-famous jockeys—and their horses? She shook her head. Her bangs fell over one eye.

A moment later, with toothpaste fuzzing around her

mouth, she checked her face again. Nope, no change. She spit and rinsed.

"You about done in there?" Rhonda, of the carrot-red mop, hammered on the door.

"Do you know who you're yelling at?" Trish opened the door and leaned against the frame. A grin attacked the corners of her mouth and winked in her hazel eyes.

"The winner of the Santa Anita Derby." Rhonda pretended boredom just before she grabbed Trish in a bear hug and danced her around the room. The two girls flopped back on the bed. "You really did it! You and Spitfire showed 'em all." They stared up at the ceiling. "So now what?"

"Now we rush downstairs and meet my dad."

"No, silly." Rhonda punched her on the arm. "Do you go for the Triple Crown, or what?"

Trish let the question sink in. "I wish I knew," she whispered. "I just wish I knew."

———

Reporters met them at Spitfire's stall. After all the questions and pictures right after the race, Trish was surprised to learn there were more to come. She left them to her father while she measured the grain for Spitfire's morning feed. She'd already realized that the tall, ebony colt hid her from the inquisitive journalists.

"So, how does it feel?" her curly-haired brother David asked as he picked Spitfire's hooves.

"I'll tell you when I figure it out." Trish kept on brushing.

It seemed only moments later that she and her father Hal were waving goodbye to Rhonda, David, and her mother. They were driving home to Vancouver, Washington.

Marge kissed her husband and hugged Trish. "You two drive carefully now." Her chronic worrying always stole some of a day's happiness from Trish.

"Don't worry, Mom." Trish halfheartedly returned her hug. She and her mother didn't see eye to eye about a lot of things, like Trish driving the big horse van or racing thoroughbreds.

Trish rubbed her forehead. A headache thumped behind her eyes. She finished packing for the return home.

"You about ready?" Her father massaged her shoulders.

Trish let her head drop forward. She took a deep breath and relaxed under his ministering fingers. "Yeah, anytime you are."

"We'll fill that ice pack one more time, as soon as we load Spitfire." Hal dug out the tension in her neck with his thumbs. Spitfire leaned over the green-web harness across the stall opening and nuzzled her hair. When she didn't respond, he lipped a curl in her bangs, and tugged.

"Ouch!" Trish shoved the black nose away. "You did that on purpose!" Spitfire rolled his eyes in mock fright. He blew in her face, then rubbed his forehead against her chest, begging for the scratching she performed so well.

"We should form a line here." Trish stroked her horse's neck while her father finished smoothing the knots of tension from her own.

"You need anything else then?" Brian Sweeney, long-time friend of Hal's who had invited them to stable in his barn at the track, asked in his slight Canadian accent.

"Just more ice after we load this guy." Hal clipped a

lead shank to Spitfire's halter. "Here, Tee, take him up."

Trish led the colt out the open entry of the green stables and to the foot of the loading ramp of their borrowed horse van. Spitfire didn't even hesitate this time when his feet thudded on the padded ramp. He followed her right up.

"Good fella." Trish knotted the half-hitch to hold him in place while her father velcroed the canvas ice pack to the colt's right foreleg. The knee had been warm ever since the race, but at least it wasn't hot and swollen like times in the past. If it didn't heal in the next few weeks, a hot knee could keep them from the Kentucky Derby the first Saturday in May.

Hal and Trish thanked Brian one more time before climbing into the truck and buckling up. Hal put the rig in gear and eased down the hard-packed dirt road to the gate. The guard waved them through.

"We'll be back," Hal promised as they followed the curving street back to the freeway. Trish turned for a last glimpse of the imposing green Santa Anita grandstand. Straight ahead it looked as if they were driving smack into the San Gabriel mountains. One more look back and all she saw were the tall spindly palm trees that decorated the in-field. Santa Anita certainly had an aura all its own. What would Churchill Downs, home of the Kentucky Derby, be like?

By the time they hit I–5, Trish was deep into her history book. She should have studied more while at the track, but since it was spring break, she only had a couple of days' assignments to do.

The first day they drove as far as Adam Finley's stunning ranch in the foothills above Harrisburg. They stopped there on their way south, and the Finleys already seemed like old friends to Trish, too. She sucked in her breath again at the Spanish splendor of the breeding farm. It seemed strange to see roses blooming already, but the scarlet-covered plants lining the exterior fences didn't know that it was barely spring in Washington state.

The two Rottweiler dogs announced the truck's arrival and just like before, former-jockey, now renowned-trainer, Adam Finley directed them to park and showed them to the stable.

"Ah, I see you're havin' a bit o' leg trouble." He pointed at the pack covering Spitfire's knee.

"It's getting to be a chronic thing with him," Hal said as Trish led the colt down the ramp. "It's been worse before."

Trish halted the horse so her father could remove the wrap. "I'll just walk him around a bit to loosen both of us up."

"I'm thinking you better not let him loose in the paddock this time," Adam suggested. "He might jump and strain that knee even more. Soon as you're done, Trish, there're cold drinks and dinner up at the house. Martha's been looking forward to your coming."

Trish walked Spitfire a good half hour before she let him loose in a stall deeply bedded with straw. She velcroed the newly-filled ice pack around his leg and gave him a last pat as he buried his nose in the grain bucket. "Pig out, fella, you earned it." Spitfire blew molasses-smelling grain in her face and went back to his meal. "Thanks." She wiped the mixture of grain and slobber off her nose. "I needed that."

She reached down and petted the two black and tan dogs that met her at the stable entry. They gamboled in front of her, darting back for more ear scratchings and nipping at each other to get her attention. Trish laughed. This was like home, only their collie Caesar had a lot more hair.

Trish took a deep breath as she strode up the brick walk to the stucco ranch house. Curved arches shaded the entry and served as a trellis for flaming bougainvillea. On the trip down, she'd learned that the sweet smell came from the orange trees lining the sides of the house. She also remembered the swimming pool in the back yard. Maybe she could get a dip in before they left in the morning.

"I have a proposition for you," Adam Finley said after they'd finished a barbecued steak dinner. "How'd you like to come down here and ride for me this summer? I know your season up there will be done by the end of April, and after the races back east and school's out, you could bring some of your string down here." He nodded at Hal. "Then she could ride for both of us."

Trish stared from the rosy-cheeked man to her father and back again. "I—ah—it would—ah . . ." She had no idea what to say. This would for sure be a chance to build a reputation in the big leagues. And their horses were every bit as good as those in California. Spitfire had just proved it. She raised stricken eyes to her father. What would her mother say about something like this? She'd just as soon her daughter quit racing altogether. Trish sighed. Her mother would *never* let them do this.

"Thanks for the vote of confidence," Hal said as he leaned his chair back. "Marge and I'll have to give this some thought. You know, with this bout of cancer and all the chemotherapy treatments, I have a hard time being away from home much, and, well, Marge isn't too excited about Trish's racing as it is." He rubbed his chin. "I had thought about coming down for a race or two."

Trish stared at him in astonishment. He'd not mentioned to her about coming back to California so soon.

"The purses are better than Longacres in Seattle, and since they're going to tear that track down, the only other races up in our neck of the woods are Yakima and the county fairs," Hal continued.

"Besides that, man, your colt has put you up in the big leagues. You'd be doing him an injustice not to race him again with horses of equal caliber," Adam reminded him.

"I know," Hal agreed.

"On top of that, it would be wonderful to have a young girl around again," Martha added. "We've plenty of room for you in our condo in San Mateo." She patted Trish's hand. "I'd promise your mother to take good care of you."

"Thank you," Trish said. Her smile didn't begin to relay the pleasure she felt at the warm invitation. Just think, living in California for the summer.

Don't think about it, her little nagger said. *You know it's impossible. Remember, you have chemistry to make up, too.*

The next morning in the truck, Trish felt cranky and out-of-sorts. She knew it was the letdown after all the excitement, but that didn't help much. A nap did though.

———

"Bay Meadows sounds wonderful," Trish broke the long silence the next morning after their overnight in Ashland.

"Don't get your hopes up."

"I know. Mom won't . . ."

"Trish, she can't help her worrying. You know as well as anyone that we're involved in a dangerous business."

"And *she* doesn't think *her* daughter should be racing." Trish felt the resentment dig at her good mood. *I'll never tell my kids to be careful,* she promised herself.

"You finished your homework?"

"Now you sound like Mom." She caught the puzzled look her father sent her. This time it was a good thing he couldn't always read her mind.

"Just thought maybe you'd like to drive."

Little fingers of guilt pinched her. She *should* have noticed he was getting tired rather than sitting there griping. They made good time though, arriving home about 3:00 P.M. on Tuesday.

It felt good to be home.

Brad, David's best friend, who worked for Runnin' On Farm, and Rhonda drove in just as Trish led Spitfire into his stall after a walk that loosened them both up.

"Hi, guys," Trish flashed them a grin as she unsnapped the lead shank. "You didn't waste any time getting home from school, did you?"

"Look who's talking." Rhonda threw her arms around her friend. "How was the trip?"

"Rhonda's described the race in *detail,*" long, lean Brad said. "And I've read all the newspaper articles, which I kept for you. Now I want to hear *your* version. *And* answer the *big* question."

Perpetual-motion Rhonda couldn't keep still another minute. "When do you leave for the Derby?"

Brad gave her a pained look. "No, that's not it. Are you going for the Triple Crown?"

Trish shrugged. "Dad says take it one step at a time.

He'll decide on the other two only if we win the Derby."

"Not *if*. When." Rhonda poked Brad in the side. "We—none of us, nobody says 'if.' We only say 'when.' Trish and Spitfire are going to *win* the Kentucky Derby. No doubt about it."

That night in bed, Trish wished she could feel more secure about the big race. "All I can do is ask You to help us," she prayed. "You know everything that can happen between here and there. Please keep Dad healthy and make his next treatment go easily. And we can't go if Spitfire's leg isn't all right, so please take care of that, too." She thought for a time. "Thank you for a safe trip home and for the win. Father, help change my mother's mind about my racing. Help her quit worrying so much. Thanks. Amen."

When she thought back to the evening just passed, she hugged a happy glow to herself. Marge had made a wonderful homecoming dinner and they'd talked about the trip, the race, and the people in California—everything except the proposal from Adam Finley. She knew her father would choose the best time and place for that. However, she'd had to bite her tongue to keep from blabbing to the other three musketeers down at the barn.

Wednesday morning she was back in the groove, nearly late to school. She rushed in the main door and skidded to a stop. "On to the Kentucky Derby" proclaimed a banner strung between two posts. Another one across her locker said she was "#1 Rider." Trish folded that one and struggled with her combination lock. The bell rang before she got her books switched, so she was late to class. English Lit stood as a body and applauded.

Trish could feel the heat all the way from her toes to

the top of her head. "Thanks," she croaked as she slid into her desk.

That afternoon she received a standing ovation when her name was announced as a jockey at Portland Meadows. She was riding to the post on her first mount and could feel the waves of approval wash over her from the grandstands. She raised her whip in the air and waved, thankful for the brisk wind blowing the heat away from her face.

All the jockeys she'd met offered their congratulations and best wishes for the first Saturday in May. Genie Stokes, who sometimes rode for Runnin' On Farm, summed it up in the dressing room: "We're all rooting for you," she said. "Your dad has worked long and hard for this chance. It couldn't happen to a nicer guy, and his daughter is no slouch."

It didn't hurt to win two races and place in a third, either. Trish hurried home to work the horses there. David and Brad had already taken care of them all, even contrary Gatesby.

"And we didn't get any new bruises," Brad bragged as they walked back up the rise to his blue Mustang.

"How's Spitfire's leg?" Trish leaned down to scratch the insistent Caesar as she asked.

"Still warm as soon as he walks on it much," David answered.

"Did you lead him with Dan'l?" He was the horse that had trained her as she exercised him.

"No, just walked him around the area. Dad said to take it real easy, not even let him out in the pasture."

"Well, we gotta go. See you guys." Brad and Rhonda slammed their car doors shut. Trish and David waved goodbye and turned toward the house.

"How's Firefly?" Trish reached her arms above her head and stretched to pull the tiredness out of her muscles.

"No swelling. Hasn't been any for some time."

"Wouldn't it be something to take her to Kentucky with us, to run the Oaks?" Trish leaned against the deck railing. "I wonder if Dad's thought about that at all?"

"He said she was done for this year because of the shin problem."

"I know. But she is such a great horse, and the Oaks runs the day before the Derby. It's only for three-year-old fillies. She hasn't really had a chance to prove what she can do."

"Trish, don't get any off-the-wall ideas."

"Well, it's worth thinking about." She shoved open the sliding glass door. "And talking about." She heard retching coming from her father's bedroom. *I forgot!* The thought tore at her. *Dad's sick from his treatment and all I could think about was my day—my wins. What kind of daughter am I?* She tiptoed into the darkened bedroom.

Hal lay with one hand across his forehead. His eyes flickered open when he heard Trish whisper his name. "I'm doing okay," he said. He reached again for the basin on a chair beside his bed. The biting odor of bile from his dry heaves made Trish swallow and wish she hadn't bothered him.

Sure you are, her thoughts jeered at his words. *You're just fine and dandy.*

Hal wiped his mouth and smiled past the green tinge to his face. "Really, Tee. This time isn't anything like the last one. I'll be up and going by tomorrow. Now, tell me about your day. I hear there was a surprise waiting for you at school. And how did you do at the track?"

Trish filled him in, her excitement returning as she told him each detail. She paused at the end and licked her bottom lip. "Have you thought about taking Firefly with us to Kentucky?"

"You never quit, do you?" Hal patted his daughter's hand.

"Well, it wouldn't be a whole lot more expensive to take two horses."

"No, just plane fare, entry fees . . ."

Trish heard him but continued, "It's just a shame she's never raced against horses as good as she is, and since she missed out on Santa Anita . . ."

"Dinner's ready," Marge called from the kitchen.

"Go eat." Hal turned on his side.

When Trish checked on him later, he was sound asleep.

Trish had five mounts for Saturday's program. That was after morning works at Runnin' On Farm. Her father had surprised—and thrilled—her when he told her to gallop Firefly also. He'd been up and around, just like he promised.

"Don't get your hopes up," he'd said when Trish grinned down at him from the dark filly's back. "Let's see what happens."

Even though they didn't have a horse running that day, Marge and Hal drove Trish to the track.

"Meet you at the front gate after your last ride," Marge said. "We'll all go out for dinner."

Trish nodded and grinned her agreement, then dog-trotted off to the dressing room.

The sun kept ducking behind clouds coming from the west as though afraid to be seen too long in one place. Trish thought of the constant warmth of California as she snapped the rubber bands around her cuffs to keep the cold wind from blowing up her silks. The track was wet but not muddy.

"Be careful on that far turn," owner Bob Diego said as he gave her a leg up for the second race of the day. "Keep off the rail, it's worse there."

Trish nodded. She leaned forward and stroked the neck of her mount.

"And Trish, I cannot tell you how pleased I am for you and your father. You rode an excellent race."

"Thank you. I still get excited when I think about it."

Trish again felt the warmth of his words as she moved the horse into the starting gates. All the animals seemed keyed up. She had to back her mount out and come into the gate a second time. But the horse broke cleanly and surged to a secure spot in second. Trish held him there until the last furlong of the short race, moved up on the lead and with hand and voice encouragement, swept under the wire ahead by a length.

She won the next one for Jason Rodgers also.

"We missed you," the tall, always-perfectly-dressed Rodgers told her in the winner's circle. "But we're sure proud of you. Not many riders make a mark like you did down south. And thanks for a good win today. Meet you here again in an hour or so?"

Trish grinned at him. "Sounds good to me." And that's exactly what she did. She and another Rodgers' horse won the fifth.

"Looked like you had a bad time on that far turn," Rodgers said after the pictures had been taken and the horse led away to the testing barn.

"Yeah, we got caught on the rail and bumped around a little. The maintenance crew needs to work that spot some more."

Trish stood in line for the scale after changing silks again.

"So how does it feel to be back after a win like the Santa Anita?" veteran jockey Phil Snyder asked her.

"Cold." Trish hugged her saddle closer. "I loved the sun down there."

"And winning?" Laugh lines crinkled around his eyes.

"You should know." Trish grinned back at him. She leaned closer to whisper, "I loved every minute of it, even when I was terrified at going against the big-name jockeys. You couldn't exactly call them friendly but," she shrugged, "I met Shoemaker. And beating the others— well—"

"You can't wait to do it again." They laughed together.

"How's your new baby?" Trish asked as they walked toward the saddling paddock.

"Growing like a weed," Phil said. "I'll have him up on a horse before you know it."

Trish felt the tension in her mount as soon as she approached the saddling stall. She knew this was the first race for the colt because she'd talked to the owner earlier. The horse tossed his head and rolled his eyes when Trish reached to stroke his neck.

"Easy, fella," she crooned to him. "You don't have to act this way. Come on now." The colt stamped his foot but calmed as she kept up her easy monologue. When she mounted, she could feel him arch his back as if to buck. She stroked his neck, murmuring all the while. "You certainly live up to your name, don't you?" She gathered her reins and nodded at the owner. Spice of Life couldn't have been more descriptive.

"Watch him closely," the trainer said as he handed

the lead shank over to the woman riding the horse that would parade them to the post. "And you be careful, Trish."

Trish felt the horse settle down about halfway to the post, and when they cantered back toward the starting gates, he quit fighting the bit. His gait smoothed out, so she didn't feel like she was riding a pile driver.

"That's a good fella," she sang to the flicking ears. "Whoops! Not so good! Whoa now!" Her commands seemed to spin off into thin air as the frightened colt backed out of the gates as fast as he should have been breaking forward. The handler led him back in.

Spice of Life snorted and shook his head. Trish settled herself in the saddle. She'd almost been ready to bale off.

"Come on, fella, let's concentrate on running, not tearing things up." The horse seemed to finally hear her and stopped shifting around.

"Good job, Trish," Snyder said from the stall to her right.

"Thanks." Trish concentrated on the space between the horse's ears. Now to get him running straight. The gates swung open and the colt hesitated before he lunged forward. His stride was choppy, so Trish held him firm to give him a chance to catch his balance.

When she finally had him running true, the field was bunched in front of them. As they rounded the first turn, Trish caught the six horses running together. When she tried to swing the colt around the outside, he fought her. He checked, stumbled, gained his feet again.

At that same moment a horse somewhere in front

broke down. As he crashed, a second horse fell over him. Bodies flew every which way. Spice of Life smashed into the screaming and kicking mass of downed horses and riders. Trish felt herself flying through the air.

CHAPTER 2

Relax! flashed from Trish's mind to her body. By now it had to be a conditioned response, or it wouldn't have happened in that split-second of catapult time.

She struck the ground at the same time her mount did. The screams of horses and humans echoed in her ears as she plowed through the soft dirt and bumped against a fallen horse's back. Then all went black.

She wasn't sure how long she'd been out. Drawing air into her lungs took major concentration. She wiggled her fingers and toes, doing a body check while she waited for her head to clear. She heard someone moaning. Someone else was either cursing or praying in rapid Spanish. A horse snorted nearby.

The sound of a motor whining around the track must surely be an ambulance. It was.

Trish rolled into a sitting position but quickly dropped her head between her knees. She wasn't sure which was worse, a rolling stomach or a woozy head.

"Just stay where you are," a male voice ordered softly. "We'll get to you as soon as we can."

While it seemed like forever, it was only a minute or so before Trish could open her eyes and focus on the carnage around her. A horse lay just beyond her feet. It must have been what she bumped against. It hadn't moved.

Trish swallowed—hard.

She looked up to see the EMT's, Emergency Medical Technicians, loading a covered stretcher into the ambulance. *Covered!* The thought flashed through her own misery. Was someone dead? Two others were working over a jockey who groaned when they moved him.

By the outside rail, a horse stood, head down, not putting any weight on a front leg. Trish could see blood running from the open gash caused by a compound fracture.

She gritted her teeth. They'd probably have to put that horse down.

"Just take it easy," a voice from behind her said. "We have another ambulance on the way."

"I'm fine." Trish turned her head very carefully so her stomach would stay down where it belonged. "I don't need an ambulance."

"Why don't you let us be the judge of that?" The first ambulance pulled away, lights flashing. "Now, any pain here?" The blond-haired young man pressed on her legs.

Trish swallowed again. She spit out some of the track dirt. When she lifted her hands to remove her helmet, the world spun around like an out-of-control carousel.

"Take it easy and let me help you." The blue-uniformed man squatted in front of her, still checking her arms and legs. He finished unbuckling her helmet and handed it to her. "Now, how's the head?"

"Hurts, but not bad. I just feel dizzy when I move." Trish ran her fingers over the dent in the side of her helmet. Someone had kicked her—big time. No wonder she felt funny.

"Let's get you on a back board and brace your neck for the ride in, just in case you've broken something in your neck or spine." The EMT smiled at her as another person brought over the equipment.

"Do I have to?" Trish pleaded. "I've been through this before. I'm okay, really." She kept insisting but didn't have the strength to fight them, especially since every time she moved her head, the world tilted.

The ride to the hospital was mercifully short. The worst part was the lump of dirt digging a hole in her left hip. Once she'd removed that, the rest of the ride was fairly comfortable.

"How bad is she?" Marge asked as the attendants pulled the gurney out of the ambulance. Her voice sounded rigid, as if she had to force her words from between clenched teeth.

"Hi, Mom." Trish raised her head and reached for her mother's hand. "You got here awfully fast."

"It's not hard when you're following an ambulance." Hal took her other hand. He leaned down and kissed his daughter's cheek.

Trish felt a tear slip from her eye and run down into her ear. She sniffed. "I'm okay, except for a dizzy head. Make them let me up, please. I don't want to go through X-rays and everything again."

"Just be patient." Marge clamped on to Trish's hand as if her daughter might be ripped away from her. "It's better to get checked out just—just in case—there's more."

"Mo-o-m!"

"No, she's right, Tee. We'll be right beside you," her father assured her.

The EMT's pushed the gurney through the hospital's

automatic doors and into a curtained cubicle. On three they lifted her, board and all, to a hospital gurney.

"By the way," the cheerful blond man said before he left, "you're one whale of a rider. I've been watching you since last fall and if I had a horse, I'd sure want you riding it. You take care, and good luck at the Derby."

"Thanks." Trish waved back as he left the room. She rolled her head to the side to smile at her mom and dad. One look at her mother's frozen face and Trish knew there was deep trouble. "B-b-but, Mom, this wasn't *my* fault."

"It wasn't anyone's fault, Tee." Her father squeezed her hand. "That's what your mother has always tried to tell you. Accidents—serious accidents—often happen through no one's fault, but people, and horses, can get hurt. Seriously hurt. Or even die."

Marge rubbed her arms above her elbows as if seeking some kind of warmth. Hal put his arm around her and hugged her into his side.

"Die?" Trish remembered back to the track. "That horse I fell against. It died?"

Hal nodded. The sorrow in his eyes as he kissed his wife's hair penetrated the fuzziness Trish felt when she moved her head.

"That's not all?" It was more a statement than a question.

Her father shook his head. "Phil Snyder was killed too. Broke his neck in the fall."

Marge shuddered and hid her face in Hal's shoulder.

Trish bit her lip on the cry that tore from her heart. Tears welled in her eyes and ran through the mud on her face and into her ears. She stared up at the square blocks of ceiling tile. "But—but I was just talking with him before the race—and he has a baby—and—and . . ." She didn't have the courage to look at her mother.

"Well, Trish, so you're back again. We're going to have to quit meeting this way . . ." The doctor stared from her face to Hal's. "Is she worse than they told me?" His question was low, meant for Hal's ears alone. Hal shook his head.

The doctor paused.

Tears slid silently from Trish's eyes. She clenched her fists at her sides on the narrow gurney. *Do not fall apart now! You're tough. Hang in there!* Her orders seemed to be working. She could swallow again.

"I'm sorry, Trish." The doctor picked up her hand and checked her pulse while he spoke. "Phil Snyder was a fine man, besides a good rider. That was a terrible accident." He shifted into a more professional tone. "Now let's see how you're doing. They said concussion. Your vision a bit foggy?" Trish nodded. "And movement makes it worse, right?" he answered when a grimace squinted in her eyes. "Nausea?"

"Some. But it's better now. How about just letting me go home? I'll be—I'm fine. Really, I am." Trish sniffed the offensive tears back.

The doctor moved her arms and legs, all the while asking, "Hurt here? How about here?" He checked her eyes again. "Any pain anywhere else?"

Trish took a deep breath, almost shook her head and caught herself just in time. "No, not really. Please, no X-rays. Just let me go home."

The doctor studied her for a moment. "Does this feel any different than the last concussion you had? Now be honest with me, Trish. You know what that other concussion felt like, and I can't find anything else."

"About the same. I don't feel like running track right now, but Dad's always said I have a hard head. Guess this just shows he's right."

The doctor rubbed his chin. He extended his hand. "Well, let's get you upright and see how you do. Easy now." He helped her sit up and swing her legs to the side.

Trish gulped and squeezed her eyes shut. She took a deep breath, slowly raised her head and swallowed again. The room stayed in one place. Her mother and father didn't fade in and out like before.

The doctor nodded. "You'll call if you notice anything different?"

"Yes." She kept her head still. She'd learned that trick pretty quickly.

"We'll have the nurse wheel you out." He shifted his attention to Trish's parents. "Call me if you need me?" He studied Marge's pale, set face. She hadn't said a word throughout the examination.

Trish saw him glance from Marge to Hal, a question on his face. Marge looked like she'd shrunk. Her shoulders, arms, and neck seemed squeezed inward as if she were trying to disappear. When the doctor touched her shoulder, she flinched and tucked her face into Hal's shoulder again.

"We'll be fine," Hal answered the unspoken question. "I'll get them both home and to bed. We've had a pretty big shock today." He turned toward the curtain opening. "We'll get the car."

"I can give her something," the doctor said. "Make it easier."

Hal smoothed a gentle hand over his wife's hair. "I'll let you know." Marge seemed to shuffle as they left.

Trish wanted to scream, but instead she asked the

question quietly: "What's wrong with my mother?"

"An accident like this can cause shock to family members, too. Besides, you've all been through a lot these last months. Sometimes the body needs a break."

"That's all?"

"That's plenty. You'll call me if you feel worse?"

Trish nodded as she allowed the doctor and nurse to help her into the wheelchair. "Thanks."

"Yeah, changing altitude'll get you. Let me know now," the doctor patted her hand. "About your mom, too."

Silence filled the car on the way home. Trish lay down in the back seat, her head resting on her bent arm. The last she heard were the tires howling across the metal treads on the I–5 bridge across the Columbia River.

"Come on, sleepyhead, we're home." Her father patted her shoulder gently.

Trish sat up very carefully. "Where's Mom?"

"I already took her into the house and put her to bed. That seemed the best thing to do." Hal extended his hand to help Trish from the car.

"Why? Dad, what's really wrong with her?"

"Shock, I think. She'll be okay."

As Trish slowly changed altitudes, Hal put his arm around her shoulders so she could lean against him. Together they mounted the steps to the front door, with Trish feeling like stopping at each level. She tightened her jaw and kept on, in spite of the woozies attacking her head.

Never had her bed looked more inviting. Hal folded back the covers, then pulled off Trish's boots. "Now, you call me if you need anything else," he said.

"Where's David?"

"He and Brad are down at the barns. I'm going down to tell them what happened and check on our animals, then I'll be right back. You just get some sleep so you feel better."

"What about the horses I'm riding tomorrow?"

"First of all, you're not riding tomorrow. Give me the owners' names later and I'll call them."

"Who rode my last mount today?" Trish could feel her attention slipping.

"I'm not sure. We left right after the accident."

"Oh." His comment brought the sounds and feelings cascading back.

After he left, Trish slipped out of her silks and under the covers. The bed welcomed her battered body. *I need a shower—bad.* She was asleep before she could dwell on the thought.

Screaming horses. Groaning people. Ambulance sirens. Trish jerked awake. She took a deep breath and let her gaze rove around her room. Light from the mercury yardlight cast shadows across the floor. It had been a dream, but the dream mirrored reality. Tears started again. Phil was dead—what about his family? Horses were killed. She'd never heard even the oldtimers talk about an accident as bad as this one.

"Oh, God, thank you for taking care of me out there." She stopped the prayer. *Why me? Why did Phil die and not me? Who makes the choices? And why? It all happened so quickly—and so senselessly. None of it makes any sense.* She tried to shut out the thoughts. But when she clenched her eyes closed, the pain in her head came back.

Her little nagging voice snuck by her resolve: *Now you know why your mother worries so much. No matter how well you ride, an accident can happen.*

Trish wished the voice would go back to sleep. She wished *she* could go back to sleep. "And Jesus, please help my mom. I know she is hurting too. And the Snyder family, help them and all the others hurt in that mess. Thanks again. Amen." She pulled the covers back up to her chin, and slept.

Trish felt the bathroom urge sometime in the dark hours before dawn. As she passed her parents' bedroom, she heard them talking.

"I can't take any more," her mother said between gut-wrenching sobs. "It could have been Trish out there. She *was* out there."

Trish could hear her father's soothing murmur.

"I—just—can't—take—any more!"

Trish slipped into the bathroom and quietly shut the door.

It's all your fault, she heard her nagger accusing her.

It was light out when she staggered up to go to the bathroom again. If she took things easy, it wasn't so bad. She nearly freaked when she looked in the mirror. She hadn't washed her face, and mud from the track still outlined where her goggles had been, and smeared across her cheeks and chin. She scrubbed a wet wash-cloth across the worst of it and went back to bed. The house was strangely silent for the 8:00 A.M. that the clock read.

Maybe she'd dreamed that her parents talked in the night. *I hope so,* she thought. *What if they make me quit racing?*

Hunger pangs woke her at ten. She entered an empty kitchen after a careful walk down the hall. One thing was sure, she felt much better than last night. But where was everybody? Had they left for church without telling her? She poured cold cereal and milk into a bowl and sat down at the table. After the cereal and a piece of toast, she searched for a note by the phone. None.

She looked out the window at the driveway. All the cars were parked in their normal places, so Dad and David must be down at the barn. Shivering, she headed back to her bed. On the way she opened the closed door and glanced into her parents' bedroom. In the darkened room, a mound raised the covers on her mother's side of the bed.

Trish stopped at the door. "Mom?" No answer. What could be happening? Her mother never slept late. She was always the first one up because she loved early mornings. And to miss church? Could something really be wrong with her mother?

CHAPTER 3

"Is Mom sick?" Trish confronted her father when he walked in the door.

"Well—" Hal took the time to hang up his coat before replying. "That depends on what you call sick. She doesn't have the flu or a cold."

"So?"

"I think she just needs some time out."

"Because of the accident?"

"That, and all the rest of the stress that's been going on around here." Hal sank into his recliner and patted the hearth beside him. "Sit down, Tee. Maybe you can help me with some ideas."

Trish sat down very carefully, because changing altitudes still caused her stomach to flip. Besides, she sported a couple of bruises from where she'd hit the ground. She stared at her father, waiting for him to quit fidgeting and begin. *Please, please, don't let him ask me to quit racing*, she pleaded to her Heavenly Father.

"I think we have to give your mother the kind of care she's always given us."

Trish clenched her eyes shut and gritted her teeth. *He can't ask me to quit. He just can't!* She opened her eyes again. Tears burned behind her eyelids.

"I know you don't feel too well, but if you start the

dinner, I'll help you with it."

Dinner! The word smacked into her brain and exploded in red, white and blue streamers. *Dinner!* She released the streamers in a laugh and a hug. "Sure, Dad. I'd be glad to."

Trish felt like dancing into the kitchen. She was dancing in her mind even though she walked carefully. She stared into the freezer. Yep, she could thaw and fry the chicken. Potatoes—her dad could peel those; there were plenty of vegetables, corn would be good. All the while one part of her mind thought *dinner,* the other rejoiced. She'd still be racing!

But by dinner her mother hadn't come out of her room. She refused a tray; said she wasn't hungry. While Trish and her father had a good time making the dinner, it just wasn't right. Her mom had always been there. If she'd been gone—but that was the problem, she wasn't gone. She was right in the bedroom, and Dad said she wasn't really sick.

David didn't have a lot to say at dinner, either. No one did.

"How's Spitfire's leg?" Trish looked at David.

"Uh, better."

"The ultrasound is helping?"

"I guess."

Hal stared at his dinner. "Thanks, Tee." He shoved the half-full plate away. "Sorry, but guess I'm not too hungry after all. Think I'll go sit with your mother for a while."

A knock changed his direction from the hall to the front door. "Why, Pastor Mort. How good to see you. Come on in, we were just finishing dinner. Can we get you a cup of coffee?"

Trish started to leap up, but stopped mid-jump and

pushed herself up slowly. "Quick, David, clear the table. I'll put the coffee on and . . ."

The two men entered the dining room.

"How are you, Trish?" Pastor Mort extended his hand. "I heard you were part of that horrible accident yesterday." He squeezed her hand and patted her shoulder. "Had to come myself to make sure you were okay. Hi, David. It's good to see you." He glanced into the kitchen. "Marge around?"

"Have a seat," Hal said. "I'm glad you came by."

Trish picked up her dishes and escaped to the kitchen. "I'll get some coffee going." She listened to the friendly talk with one ear, kept her hands busy filling the coffeepot with water, and still had time to think that she looked worse than a drowned rat. At least she'd taken a hot shower, which got the kinks loosened up and the dirt off her face. But she was wearing the gross sweats she'd worn when her arm was broken. She set out mugs and arranged peanut butter cookies on a plate. As soon as the coffeemaker stopped gurgling, Trish carried the tray of refreshments into the dining room.

"Thanks, Trish." Pastor Mort smiled at her when she handed him a mug of coffee. "Black, just the way I like it."

"You're welcome." Her smile slipped a little as her nagger reminded her she'd forgotten to ask if he took cream and sugar. Her mother didn't forget things like that. *She* should be out here. "Dad, anything else?" She set his mug on the table.

The twinkle in her father's eyes told her he knew *exactly* what she was thinking. "Thanks, Tee."

"Well, I'd better get down to the barn and start chores." David snagged a cookie off the plate as he stood up. "Good to see you, Pastor."

Trish started to clear more dishes from the table, then stopped. Maybe if she got out of there, the two men could talk about how to help her mom. Maybe Pastor Mort could get Marge to come out of her room. "I'll be down in a minute," she told David.

"There's plenty more coffee," she said as she picked up the bowls of leftover food.

"You ready for the big one?" Pastor Mort asked.

"Hope so. If Spitfire's leg gets better, and if—" she glanced at her father. "Or, rather, when." Hal grinned at her. "I have to keep reminding myself that 'if' doesn't count." Trish smiled back at the contagious grin on her pastor's face. She was quoting his own words.

"Good for you, Trish." The balding man nodded as he spoke. "You've got the right attitude, and I know it hasn't come easily."

"Thanks. See you later."

Trish grabbed some carrots from the fridge before she went out the door, and broke them into pieces on her way to the barn. Caesar met her halfway, barking his approval and begging for attention. Trish slapped her chest with both hands and the dog responded by planting his forefeet by her hands. Trish scratched his ears and tugged on the white ruff.

"You ol' sweetie." Her nose got a quick lick. Then her chin. "Hey, knock it off. I washed my face today." Caesar grinned his doggy grin and gave her another quick one before he dropped to the ground.

Trish took a deep breath. Nickers escalated to whinnies when her stable friends heard her voice. She heard David talking to them as he moved from stall to stall with the evening feed. A pheasant rooster called out in the field. Trish searched the fence rows toward the west, trying to locate him. Another deep breath took in the aromas of spring—growing grass, freshly turned dirt, all overlaid with a tinge of stable. She grinned down at the dog sitting at her feet. "Come on, fella, let's go see the kids."

She gave each of the racing string a bit of carrot and a quick scratch as she walked down the line. Spitfire smeared grain on her cheek as he blew in her face. Gray Dan'l begged for more—both carrots and loving. Even Gatesby acted glad to see her, a wuffle warming her fingers as he picked up his carrot.

Trish left them behind and headed for the paddock behind the old barn where the two foals played at grazing along with their dams. When she whistled, Miss Tee, the filly born on Trish's birthday in September, trotted up to the fence. She'd lost her baby coat and was deepening into a dark bay, with one white sock and a narrow blaze down her face. Double Diamond, the January-born colt, hesitated before following the filly up to the fence.

"You two are absolutely the neatest babies anywhere." Trish rubbed Miss Tee's ears and stroked down the brush of a mane. She kept an eye on Double D, waiting for him to tiptoe up. Miss Tee nudged Trish in the chest. "Knock it off, silly, pretty soon you'll be big enough to knock me over that way." Trish stroked her baby's soft nose and tickled the whiskery upper lip. Miss Tee tossed her head, then nibbled on Trish's fingers. She sniffed Trish's jacket pockets, searching for more treats.

Trish snapped a lead rope on the filly's halter, then opened the gate to do the same for the mare that ambled up for her treat. As she walked the two of them to the barn, Double D and his mother whickered their protest.

38

"I'll be back in a minute," Trish assured them.

A few minutes later, with both pairs shut in their stalls with feed and water, Trish strolled back outside. She could see David down in the pasture checking the outside stock. As she watched, he clipped a lead rope on the pregnant mare and led her up the lane. Trish turned back into the barn to prep the foaling stall.

"You think it's tonight?" she asked as David led the mare into the newly strawed stall.

"Better safe than sorry." David unsnapped the rope and gave the mare a pat on the shoulder as he eased by her. "Her milk's in and she seems kind of restless. I'll check on her a couple of times tonight."

Trish leaned her chin on her arms crossed on the top of the stall door. She studied the mare that pulled hay from the full manger and munched contentedly. "They sure are tricky, aren't they? To think a horse can stop labor at will, or even choose when to drop her foal."

"Yeah, it all helps, especially if you're wild and trying to keep away from predators."

"I know. Adam Finley had video cameras in his foaling stall, and a sound system so he could hear if the mare started panting. You should see that spread, Davey boy. It's unbelievable."

"Well, things like that would make our lives easier, too, but with only one or two foaling at a time, it would be mighty expensive."

"I know, but we can dream, can't we?"

David patted her on the shoulder. "Come on, dreamer. Say good-night to your friends and let's get out of here."

"See you two later," Pastor Mort called as they came up the rise. They waved back and watched his car move down the drive.

"You think he talked with Mom?" Trish scuffed her boot toe in the gravel.

"I sure hope so. I've never seen her like this." David tucked both hands in the back pockets of his jeans.

"Scary, huh?"

"Yeah."

"How's Mom?" Trish asked after they'd shut the door. Her father shrugged and shook his head.

When Trish stepped into the dark bedroom a while later and whispered, "Mom?" there was no answer. She left quietly, wishing she could say or do something that would help.

Trish had barely closed her eyes after her prayers, when the nightmares rolled over her again. She felt herself flying through the air. "Oh!" She jerked upright. Blinking her eyes, she tried to clear both her vision and her head. Her mouth felt like horses had been racing through it. Her heart pounded as if she'd been the one racing.

With a sigh, she lay back down and stared up at the leafy patterns reflected on the ceiling. Shadows from the branches swaying in the breeze danced above her. Trish willed her eyes to stay open, knowing that the terrible sounds and pictures would return when she slipped into sleep.

Remember the name of Jesus, her helpful inner voice whispered. *That worked in the fog, didn't it?*

Trish smiled to herself. *That's right, it did.* It was nice to get some inner help for a change. "Jesus, Jesus." When she closed her eyes, she pictured Him sitting on a rock with children around Him. He was laughing.

She slept. In peace.

When her alarm went off, Trish stretched and

yawned. She certainly felt better than yesterday. The house was silent when she padded down the hall to the bathroom. Her parents' bedroom door was still closed.

"Hi, Tee," her father said when she peeked around the corner to the dining room table.

"Is Mom . . ."

Hal shrugged. He rubbed his forehead with his fingers as if he had a headache. "I don't know." He took a deep breath. "David's down at the barn with the mare that foaled, so I'll take you to school. It's a filly," he answered the question before she could ask. "And yes, she's fine, and no, you haven't time to go see her before school."

"You could at least let me get a word in edgewise."

"Why? Then you'd try to talk me into letting you see her."

Trish grinned at the accuracy of his statement. She thought about her mother all the time she was showering and dressing. What was going on? Her mother couldn't just check out like this, could she? Maybe she really was sick and not telling them. The thought stopped her toothbrush cold. Mom couldn't be sick, too. She just couldn't. Didn't they have enough problems with her father's cancer? Her stomach clenched, like a bad charlie horse.

———

"You taking Mom to the doctor today?" she asked just before getting out of the car at school.

"We'll see. You make sure you talk with Mrs. Olson now. You know you have to set up a homework schedule for while you're gone."

"I know." Usually the thought of the Derby made her

float about eighteen inches off the ground. Today her feet were encased in concrete. "See you." She waved as she slung her book bag over her shoulder.

By afternoon Trish had a headache of her own. The doctor had warned her about trying to read, and boy, was he ever right. Sentences jumbled together, and words—well, it was like looking through a waterfall— all blurry. Besides, so many kids had asked about the accident. She felt like a celebrity in reverse. And every time she thought about Phil and his family, the tears stung the backs of her eyes.

"Bad time, huh?" Mrs. Olson patted Trish's hand when she sat in the chair by the counselor's desk. "I can tell you're not feeling so great, so how can I help you?"

"We'll be shipping Spitfire to Kentucky about the fifteenth, and then I'll fly out there on the eighteenth. The Derby is on May 6th." Trish paused.

"And then?"

"Then, I don't know. See, the problem is no one else can ride Spitfire, so we'll decide about the other races depending upon what happens at the Derby."

"So, if you win you could miss more school?"

"I guess." Trish was having trouble concentrating. Her head had gone beyond just hurting and was now in serious pain.

"Trish, you're turning green right before my eyes. What's wrong?"

"I got a bit of a concussion on Saturday and . . ."

"And you should be home in bed." Mrs. Olson shook her head but smiled at the same time. "Why don't you go lie down in the nurse's room." She checked her watch. "The bell will ring in about half an hour. I'll let Brad know where you are."

Trish nodded—carefully. "Thanks."

"And Trish, I'll let your teachers know about our talk so they're ready to help you with a schedule."

"Bad, huh?" Rhonda said, after she and Brad walked with Trish out to Brad's baby-blue Mustang.

"Better now than a while ago." Trish slid into the front seat and dropped her head back against the headrest. The pain pills she'd taken seemed to be helping.

She opened her eyes when the car stopped in her yard. A strange car was parked beside the family sedan. "See you guys."

"I'll be back for chores in about half an hour. You aren't riding, are you?" Brad asked.

"I was planning on it, but you and David'll have to do the honors." She shut the door without a slam.

She stopped as soon as she shut the door into the house. The car belonged to Pastor Mort, and he and her parents were in the living room praying. Trish added her own "amen," greeted them, and headed for her bedroom. The bed welcomed her with open sheets. *At least Mom was sitting in her chair.* The thought flitted away as her eyelids slammed shut.

Dinner was another silent affair. "Your mother's sleeping," Hal said. Trish squelched her questions when she looked at her father's face.

"Tomorrow's the funeral." Hal looked from Trish to David. "You don't have to go if you don't want to."

"I'll go," David said.

Trish felt her stomach cramp again. "I'll go," she whispered. *But I've never been to a funeral before,* she wanted to cry out.

CHAPTER 4

"I can do all things through Christ who strengthens me." Trish repeated the verse over and over. "All things. I can do all things, even go to a funeral." *But I don't want to go. I don't want Phil to be dead.* She stared at her tear-stained face in the mirror.

Morning had come too soon. David and her father sat in the dining room eating breakfast. Marge still hadn't come out of her room. And Trish—all she wanted to do was hide her head under the pillow. If her mother could, why couldn't she?

She stuffed the thought back down where she hid the questions too hard to think about. Her mother really must be sick. What if something *was* wrong and no one was telling her? Maybe her mother had a terrible disease. Why hadn't she gone to the doctor? Another question to stuff.

"I'm so scared," she finally admitted. Bracing her arms on the counter, she let her head drop forward. So scared. So worried. *Just like my mother.*

Trish blotted her eyes and tugged the brush through her hair. Even that was harder to do now that she'd let her hair grow longer. She gritted her teeth. Obviously this was going to be one of *those* days. She *had* to talk to her mother, that was all there was to it.

When she opened the bathroom door, she could hear the men talking in the dining room. She tiptoed across the hall and knocked on her parents' door. When there was no answer, she opened it anyway and walked into the darkened room. As her eyes adjusted to the dimness, she could see her mother lying on her side facing the window.

"Mom?" She padded around the end of the bed and scrunched down beside the still form. "Mom?" A little louder this time.

Marge opened her eyes.

"Are you sick, Mom? What's wrong? Can I get you something?"

Marge shook her head. "No, just leave me here."

"But—but—you haven't eaten. You—you—we need you." Trish reached out to touch her mother's shoulder.

Marge flinched away. "I can't—I don't want to talk now." She shut her eyes again.

Trish stared at the pale face framed by limp and matted hair. "But, Mom . . ." Her words trailed off. Trish slumped back on her haunches. What were they going to do?

Tears slipped from beneath her mother's closed lashes and ran unheeded onto the pillow. Trish drew a staggery breath. The tears so close to the surface today burned her eyes and made her sniff. She chewed her bottom lip as she pushed herself to her feet. "I'll talk to you later, after the funeral." She wasn't sure if the words were a promise or a plea.

Trish shut the door behind her and headed for the kitchen. On her way past the cold, gray ashes in the fireplace, she glanced at the mantel. The carved wooden eagle she'd given her father for Christmas had become a symbol of strength for all of them. She clutched the eagle to her chest as she tiptoed back into her mother's room and set it on the nightstand where Marge couldn't miss it. Eagle's wings—if anyone needed them now, it was her mother.

"*I can do all things,*" the words kept time with her feet as she mounted the broad concrete steps to the church where the funeral was being held. She clutched her father's arm with one hand and David's with the other. Even rolling her lips together failed to stem the tears that persisted.

Flowers of various colors banked the altar and surrounded the closed casket at the front of the sanctuary. A blanket of red roses like those presented to a winning rider covered the shiny wood. Organ music floated over and under the murmur of voices from people in the packed pews. Trish recognized owners, trainers, jockeys, and stable hands. It seemed everyone connected with The Meadows was present.

The hymns, the sermon, the words spoken by Phil's friends, all passed in a blur as Trish fought her own battle against the sobs that threatened to break through. One verse stayed in her mind: "He fought the good fight, he has finished the race, he has kept the faith. Henceforth there is laid up for him a crown of righteousness . . ."

Hal handed her a handkerchief. "I brought an extra," he whispered in her ear as he wiped his eyes.

Six jockeys, all wearing silks, carried out the casket.

After the pastor spoke the final words at the cemetery, a red-coated steward raised a long brass bugle and blew the parade to the post. Trish felt like saluting. Instead, she wiped her eyes and, like the others, turned back to the cars. The women of the church had prepared a buffet luncheon for everyone.

Trish felt proud of her father as he placed their sympathy card on the table. She knew it contained a check for $2,000, the Runnin' On Farm's contribution to a fund for the grieving family. Jockeys, owners, and trainers from all over the country would send money to the fund, whether they knew the person in trouble or not. Like other jockeys, Trish donated the fee from one mount. That was the way of the track.

But her father had a reputation for helping those in need. He'd said it was his way of paying back some of the blessings God had given them. The warm glow wasn't drowned out by the tears Trish sniffed when she shook Mrs. Snyder's hand.

Back home, she changed her clothes and looked longingly at her bed. Instead of a nap she walked slowly down to the barn. She should go to school for a couple of hours, but it was too big an effort. She stopped to pat each of the stabled horses. Soft nickers and wuffles greeted her, as if they were surprised to see her.

She leaned against Spitfire's shoulder after opening the stall door and slipping inside. She wrapped both arms around his neck and rested her cheek on the coarse black mane. *"And He will raise you up on eagle's wings . . ."* The song trickled back in her mind. "I wonder," she whispered to no one in particular, "if that's what death is like?" Spitfire's ears twitched and he nuzzled her shoulder, as if to agree with her.

"God, thank you for making my dad better." She let the song continue in her mind. *" . . . and hold you in the palm of His hand."* Trish found herself humming the tune as she scratched Spitfire's ears and left the stall. The

parade to post echoed in her mind as she ambled over
to the paddock where the two foals grazed with their
dams.

"What are we going to do about Mom?" Trish confronted her father that evening after they'd had a
motherless dinner again.

"Keep praying."

Tell him you'll quit racing if it would help, her little
voice whispered in her ear.

I can't do that! another part of her cried.

Not even if it would make your mother okay again?
Trish clamped her lips together. If only covering her ears
would quell the argument.

Trish glanced up to catch the look of love and under-
standing on her father's face.

"Don't worry, Tee. It'll be okay."

Funny thing, Trish thought as she crawled into bed
that night. *Dad telling me not to worry. That's what Mom
does—worry. People can't get sick from just worrying—can
they?*

The next afternoon, mounted on her first ride since
the accident, Trish wasn't so sure. Every time she closed
her eyes, the scream of horses and humans came back
to her. She clenched her teeth to keep them from chat-
tering.

She concentrated on the trainer's instructions. "He's
really ready; you should do well today. He hates dirt in
his face, so he'll go for the front. Go to the whip if you
have to."

Trish nodded. She hated using a whip. As the parade
to post echoed over the tinny loudspeaker, her stomach

did a couple of flips. A sharp, bitter taste clawed at the back of her throat.

"You okay, Trish?" the rider on the lead pony asked.

"Yeah. Yeah, I'm fine." Trish nearly choked on the lie. She wasn't fine. She knew she'd better get control of herself or she'd never keep control of her horse.

You're afraid, her nagging voice jeered in her ear. *You're scared!*

———————

The horse jigged and snorted as the handler at the starting gates took the lead shank. When the gate clanged behind them, the horse threw up his head. Trish tightened the reins. Her voice trembled at first, but she forced herself to continue the soothing monologue. It calmed both her and the horse.

The last horse entered the starting gates. Trish focused on the spot between her mount's ears. And they were off.

Her horse paused a moment before his leap out of the gate. Then he bobbled. Trish tightened her reins to keep him on his feet. The field surged ahead of them.

"Come on, lazy bones, you're the one who doesn't like a face full of dirt." Her horse lengthened out, settling into his stride. "Come on, baby, let's make up for lost time here."

They came out of the first turn gaining on the horses bunched ahead of them. Trish saw a gap between two other mounts and aimed hers right down the slot, until they drew even.

She couldn't do it. Echoes rang in her head. Screams. Horses falling.

Trish pulled her mount back and swung out to go around.

They didn't even come in the money.

Trish could hardly look the owner and trainer in the eye. "I'm sorry." She clutched her saddle to her chest and stepped on the scale. She'd buckled.

She wanted to throw up.

CHAPTER 5

The next race wasn't much better.

"Are you all right, Trish?" owner Robert Diego asked in his precise accent. "You seem unlike your usual self."

"No, I'm fine—really." Trish clenched her hands on the reins and took another deep breath. Maybe she *should* have thrown up.

"It is sometimes difficult for a rider after a bad accident. You would tell me if this were the case?"

Trish felt the sting of tears again. Oh, if only her father were here. She swallowed. "No, no, I'm okay."

Her horse reared in the starting gate. Trish managed to stay on, but visions of getting crushed against the rear gate did nothing for her nerves. They broke bad, ran poorly, and placed sixth out of a field of eight.

Trish hated to say "I'm sorry" again, but what else could she say? The bad race wasn't really the horse's fault, even though he'd been acting erratic the entire time. Usually she could talk a horse out of that kind of behavior and get him running. That's what made her a gifted jockey. She rubbed her arms, sore from fighting with the cantankerous beast all around the track.

She didn't have a ride again until the tenth and final race of the day. *Maybe if I call Dad he can help me get over this.* She shoved the thought away. How could she tell him she was afraid?

Afraid? You're scared stiff. She heard the nagging voice accusing her again. This time he seemed to have brought his entire family to stage a shouting match in her head.

Trish exited through the front glass doors of The Meadows and angled across the asphalt parking lot. The voices kept pace with her marching feet.

Scaredy cat! Scaredy cat!

Now I know what my mother feels like.

If you were a REAL Christian you'd let God take care of this.

Worry and fear are really the same thing.

The Bible says don't be afraid.

Trish clenched her hands over her ears. Her father always said God could take care of things, but if that were so, why was her mother sick in bed? Was *she* scared to death? Were this yucky stomach and shaky hands what her mother felt when she watched her daughter ride?

Trish held her hands out in front of her. She couldn't stop the trembling. She couldn't ride another horse this way. Turning, she stared across the acres of cars to the front of the grandstand. She couldn't let another owner down. She'd have to go back in there and tell Jason Rodgers he needed to find another rider.

"No!" the cry tore from her heart. "God, please help me. I can't get back up and I don't want to chicken out." She looked around. She was alone with her tears. Trish kept on walking, the sobs shaking her shoulders. *Please help me. You promised You would.*

Remember the fog? a soft voice whispered.

Trish nodded. She thought about the guardian-angel trucker who'd turned off the fog-bound freeway at the exit that led to their motel on their trip to Santa Anita.

She leaned against a parked car and closed her eyes, picturing the verses printed on 3 × 5 cards and pinned to the wall above the desk in her bedroom. *"I will never leave you nor forsake you."*

"If you mean that, Lord, how come I feel so alone? How come I was so scared?"

"Behold I am with you always, even to the end of the age."

Boy, I feel like the end's here right now. She wiped the tears away. *It feels like I'm broken in pieces, scattered all over the place. Maybe Mom would be all right if I'd just quit racing. She's never had problems like this before, but how can I quit?*

An old familiar song floated through her mind, like a wind chime in a gentle breeze. *"Jesus loves me, this I know . . ."*

Trish raised her head and looked around her. It was so real she thought a stereo must be playing.

"God, I know You are real. And I know You hear me. I don't know what's going to happen but—well—You've been there for me in the past so I guess You'll be there for me now." She looked up as if expecting a cloud to open. It didn't.

She held out her hands. No shaking. She swallowed. Her stomach stayed down.

Trish jogged back to the grandstand, yanked open the door, and strode back to the women jockey's room.

Enveloped in the steamy hubbub, she mentally chanted the verses as she wrapped both arms around her shoulders and rounding her back, pulled the tension out. The chant continued as she dropped forward from the waist and hugged her knees.

"You okay, Trish?" Genie Stokes sat down on the bench beside her. Genie, a veteran rider of ten years, rode for Runnin' On Farm when Trish couldn't.

"I am now." Trish unclipped her hair and tousled it with her fingers. As she massaged her scalp, she glanced sideways at the woman beside her. "I—I really was scared." The words came haltingly.

"It hits the best of us. Mine was after I broke my collarbone in a really bad fall." Genie patted Trish's shoulder. "Besides, sometimes a little fear is a healthy thing. Keeps you from making stupid mistakes."

"Yeah, but this is more than a little fear." Trish turned to look at her friend. She paused. "Ah—when you've been scared—um—did you ever—ahh—" Trish cleared her throat. Her voice dropped. "I went around out there, I couldn't drive down between two other horses and the opening was big enough for a truck."

"So?"

"So we didn't even get in the money and we should have. *I* lost the race for that horse, that owner."

"Okay. You made a mistake. You were scared. But you're smart enough to talk about it. I'll bet dollars to doughnuts you'll think about this again, but you'll go on and do what you know is right. Being afraid, especially after a terrible accident like we had here, isn't a crime. It doesn't say you're a bad rider or you failed." Genie held out her hand. "Welcome to the real world of racing."

Trish dug up her sleeve for a tissue and blew her nose. "Thanks, Genie." She glanced up at the round clock on the wall. "I gotta get out there. I'm up again in the tenth."

They won. By a nose, even after being caught in the

pack up the backstretch. Trish slid off the sorrel gelding and nearly threw her arms around Jason Rodgers. She stopped herself in time to just shake his hand.

His smile felt like a hug. "I knew you could do it, Trish. You've passed a big milestone."

When Trish got home, she stopped at the closed bedroom door. She hesitated, shrugged, and then went in. "Mom."

There was no answer from the mound in the bed.

Trish sat down in the chair by the bed. She bit her lip. "Mom, you gotta get up and talk to us again. How can we help you if we don't even know what's wrong?" She waited, hoping for an answer. "I blew it today. Lost two races because I was scared." She leaned forward and touched her mother's shoulder. "Mom? Please wake up and talk to me. Get mad at me or something—anything."

Marge blinked her eyes. She stared back at Trish, then reached out to pat her daughter's hand. Her eyes drifted closed again.

Trish sighed. She shook her head and left the room. What were they going to do?

In bed that night, Trish thought back over the day. Even her mother's not talking to her didn't dampen the thrill she felt. She'd gone to the Source for help and He'd answered. She could race again.

He always answers, her little voice whispered. *You just don't like it when He says "no" or "wait."*

Trish thought about that. She turned over and snuggled the covers tight around her shoulders. So, how did you know when He said "wait"? What about her mom? Had she been praying about her worrying? Would it help if Trish quit racing? Life sure could be confusing. Her prayers that night were half thank-you's and half what-do-I-do-now's. She fell asleep with a smile on her lips.

Thursday morning on the home track, Trish rode Spitfire for the first time since Santa Anita. His leg had been cool for two days. The blue-black colt crow-hopped twice between the stable and the track. He tossed his head and danced sideways, tugging at the bit.

"Oh no you don't." Trish kept a tight rein. "You're not gonna go and mess up that knee again. We'll take this morning slow and easy. Just listen to the birds sing. See, the sun's even out for you." She took a deep breath and let it out. What a four-star, incredible morning. Green, growing spring smelled like nothing else in the world.

By the second circuit of the three-quarter-mile track, Spitfire walked flat-footed with only an occasional high-step to let off some pent-up energy. Trish settled into the saddle and leaned forward to stroke his neck.

"You leave for the Derby in less than a week—I hope," she told the twitching black ears. "So you gotta get back in shape." Spitfire nodded. Trish laughed, her joy winging away with the robin that flew from the fence after serenading them.

Thursday evening they had a family meeting—without Marge.

"I'll be honest with you kids," Hal said sadly. "I don't know what to do. The one thing I do know is that I can't go off and leave your mother while she's in this condition."

Trish stared at her hands gripped together on the table in front of her. "You mean no Derby." Once the words were out she clenched her teeth. *It just wasn't fair.* They'd worked so hard. Here her dad was better, Spitfire's leg was cool again and now this.

Hal reached over and covered her hands with one of

his. "I know how you feel, Tee. Please try not to be angry with your mother. She can't help what's going on either."

She doesn't seem to be trying too hard, Trish wanted to say but bit back the words.

"I'll be here to take care of her—of things—if you think you could go, that is," David said.

Trish looked from David to her father. Both of them looked worn down, tired.

"Thanks, David, but it wouldn't work. I couldn't concentrate on the horse when all I can think about is your mother. And Trish, if some miracle happens and we do go, I've decided to not even consider taking Firefly. We just can't handle the extra strain right now."

Trish slumped on the edge of her bed a while later. Just yesterday she'd felt as if God were really there, and now He seemed to have slipped off again. She stared at the verses on the wall. Was this a "no" or a "wait"? She sighed. She'd settle for a "wait" until it was too late to go. And a "wait" meant keep praying. So she did. Even when she woke up in the middle of the night, and the first thing when she got up in the morning, and in disjointed moments after working Spitfire. " . . . *raise you up on eagle's wings*," floated through her mind while she brushed her teeth.

"Your mom any better?" Rhonda asked when they met at their lockers before lunch.

Trish shook her head. "But something's gotta give." She told Rhonda and Brad about the meeting the night before.

"You really mad?" Rhonda asked.

"I guess. Sometimes. And other times I try not to think about it. But we keep praying." She plunked her tray down on the table. "I just know God's gonna work this out—somehow."

"You going to the track?" Brad asked around a mouthful of sandwich.

"Yeah, I have two mounts. David wants you to come help him get Final Contender loaded and over to the track. He runs in the fifth tomorrow."

"Sure. When're you working at your place?"

"We're not. After Saturday everyone is out to pasture except Spitfire. Dad says we'll think about summer racing after the Triple Crown is over. All the horses will be better off with a good rest."

When Trish got home, the pastor's car was in the drive again. He and her father were sitting in the living room talking when she stepped through the door.

"Come here for a minute, Tee." Her father motioned her over.

"Hello, Trish." Pastor Mort smiled at her.

"Hi." She looked back at her father. "What's up?"

"I—we—" Hal nodded at the serious-faced man on the sofa. "We've talked with the doctor and decided on a pretty serious course of action. There were two choices—either put your mother in the hospital or . . ."

"The hospital? Is she worse?"

"No." Hal rubbed his forehead. "Your mother has chosen the second plan. Tomorrow morning, with God and Pastor Mort's help, we'll all go to the track and talk about what happened the day of the accident."

Trish sank down on the hearth. "All of us?" Her voice squeaked on the last word. *The nightmares have finally quit. Will they start up again?*

Hal nodded. "I think it'll help you, too."

Trish shrugged. "Okay." She wet her lips. She could hear the fish tank bubbling away in the dining room. She stared at her hands clasped between her knees.

"Um-m-m, I've gotta get to the track. I've got two mounts." She rose to her feet as though she were pushing up barbells in the weight room. Her gaze flicked from one man to the other. "You're sure this is the best way?"

They both nodded.

Trish fled to her bedroom.

CHAPTER 6

Trish battled monsters all night.

"Yeah, I'm coming," she answered David's knock groggily. She could hear her brother go on down the hall. Instead of getting up, she flopped over on her back. Today they were *all* going to the track. Right after breakfast. The thought of food made her stomach turn over. What was going to happen to her mom? To all of them?

Trotting Spitfire around the track blew the cobwebs away from Trish's mind. The morning air was brisk but without the bite of winter. Spitfire tugged at the bit and every few yards danced sideways, tossing his head and snorting.

Trish laughed. "You big goof. You know I'll let you run again when you're ready. Right now, Dad says jog, so jog it is."

Spitfire shied at something only he could see.

"Knock it off." Trish automatically clamped her knees and flowed right with him. "You didn't see anything; you made it up." Spitfire snorted again. He wasn't even warm when they trotted back to the stable.

"You two looked like you were having fun," David said with a grin.

"You should have saddled Dan'l and come too."

"Naw. Need to get all this done so we can leave." He

waved at the pile of straw outside Spitfire and the gray's stalls.

His comment brought Trish back to reality with a thump. "Yeah."

"Look on the good side. This could be the thing that snaps Mom out of this." David stopped stripping the tack off Spitfire and stared at her.

"I know." Trish drew a circle in the dirt with her boot toe. Spitfire blew in her ear and nudged her shoulder. She reached up to scratch his ears and rubbed her cheek against the silky skin of the colt's cheek.

"Well?"

"Well, it's scary."

"For you or Mom?"

Trish sorted through her confused thoughts. "Probably both. I just don't want the nightmares to keep on forever."

"They won't."

"How do you know?"

"I'm your big brother. I'm paid to know these things." David handed her the saddle and bridle. "Don't worry, Tee. It'll be all right."

I wish people would quit telling me not to worry, Trish thought as she hung up the gear. *I'm not a worrier.*

Oh no? She was sure she heard her little nagger chuckle.

Her mother was up and dressed, huddled in the recliner with her eyes closed, when Trish walked back into the house after pulling her boots off at the boot jack on the deck.

"Hi, Mom." Trish started to go to her mother, then thought better of it.

Marge nodded and blinked her eyes open as if

weights had held her eyelids closed.

Trish noted the hollows in her mother's pale cheeks, the stringy hair. She changed directions and knelt by the chair. "You want me to help you wash your hair before we go? You know how much better that always makes us feel." *Come on, please. Let me help you like you always helped me.* She bit her tongue to keep the words from escaping.

The seconds seemed to stretch to hours.

Marge nodded. "If you want to."

"I'll get the towels and shampoo." Trish felt like tap dancing on the ceiling.

With her supplies in place, she walked back into the living room and picked up her mother's limp hand. "Come on." She tugged gently. "You'll feel much better." Trish felt like the parent as she led her mother by the hand into the kitchen. She adjusted the water temperature and drew the spray nozzle out.

"Lean over." Trish patted her mother's shoulder.

Marge followed Trish's orders as though she didn't have the energy to resist. "Umm-m-m," she said as Trish massaged her scalp with her strong fingers. "Feels good."

Trish felt like she'd just won the Derby. She rinsed and shampooed again. It seemed so strange to be on the giving end rather than the receiving. But it felt good.

"How about if I blow-dry it for you?" Trish asked as she toweled her mother's hair.

Marge reached up and wrapped the towel around her head. She smiled at her daughter for the first time in what seemed like months. "Okay."

Trish wielded dryer and brush like an expert. Her years of horse grooming were suddenly giving way to a new profession.

Marge closed her eyes. A deep sigh, as if from her toes, seemed to fill the bathroom and drown out the angry-bee hum of the dryer.

"You okay?" Trish stepped back to view her handi-work. She could see strands of gray that she was sure hadn't been there three weeks ago. The dark waves of her mother's hair feathered back on the sides and waved to the right on top. "You look nice." Trish held her hand over her mother's eyes and sprayed. "I think this is the first time I've ever done your hair."

"Probably." Marge sighed. "Thank you, Tee."

The ride to the track was a silent affair. Each of the family seemed lost in their own thoughts. Trish stared out the window. Her mother's eyes were closed again. She hadn't said anything since the bathroom. Her father kept darting glances at Marge, as if afraid she might back out. David chewed on a knuckle.

Trish tried to picture the verses on her wall. They were so fuzzy she couldn't read them. Good thing she knew them by heart by now. She repeated "I can do all things through Christ who strengthens me" under her breath—over and over.

The sun had gone behind the clouds by the time they parked outside the chain-link fence at Portland Mead-ows Racetrack. Golfers were still playing the nine-hole course on the infield. Morning works were over, so the tractor and drag were grooming the track. Pastor Mort's white car was parked next to a pick-up where a golf cart trundled up into the bed.

Trish felt like crawling under the seat and hiding as her father got out of the car and walked around to help Marge out. David followed his father, and between them Marge appeared smaller, as if she'd shrunk in the last week. The three of them walked toward the fence. Trish shoved open her door and stepped out. She felt anchored to the asphalt.

Pastor Mort turned, as if sensing her fear. He came over and took her arm. "Come on, Trish. It will be okay, I promise you."

Trish gritted her teeth. She *would not* cry. Together they followed the others around the outside of the track.

When they reached the spot just beyond the first turn and stopped, Pastor Mort looked at each of them. "I'd like to start with prayer." At their nods, he began, "Heavenly Father, You know how hurting we are. You made us and we are Yours. Our minds and our feelings are gifts from You and today we ask . . ."

Trish's mind tried to check out, but she clamped her jaw tight, and forced it back to the present.

" . . . that You bring healing to this family, to Hal, and Marge, to David, to Trish. You know what they need and we thank You for Your healing mercy. Amen."

Trish swallowed hard. "Amen."

"Tee, why don't you come over here by me," her father said as he reached out his arm to her.

Trish nodded. His arm felt good around her, made her think she wouldn't fly apart after all.

After a moment of silence, Pastor Mort continued. "Now Marge, I'm asking you to go back to that day, that afternoon at the track. Close your eyes and picture the track." He paused. "See the parade to the post." More silence. "See the horses enter the starting gates. Can you see it?"

Trish sensed rather than saw her mother's nod. Trish closed her eyes tighter so she could remember too.

"The horses broke from the gate and pounded in front

66

of the stands. You were down by the rail." Pastor Mort's soft voice stilled.

Trish could feel the clumps of dirt banging in to her and her mount as they came up from behind. She'd already pulled down the first pair of goggles and the second pair was darkening with dirt. She felt her mount stumble and herself flying through the air. The cry she heard wasn't from her mind.

Marge buried her face in Hal's shoulder, her sobs tearing at Trish's heart. She turned and began rubbing her mother's back. She could see the tears streaming down David's face through the waterfall of her own.

"And what do you see?" the pastor asked Marge quietly when the tears diminished.

"They've lifted Trish onto the stretcher. They've covered her face! Oh no!" Marge thumped her hand on Hal's shoulder, and the tears resumed in intensity. "They think she's dead! No! Not my Trish. No! No!"

"Mom, Mom, it's okay." Trish forced her words out around her own tears. "I'm right here. I'm all right. I didn't die. I didn't even come close to it."

"I can't handle any more. You could have died . . ." She looked up into Hal's face. "All I could see out there was Trish on a stretcher . . . and then she was in the hospital—sick—hurt. I've been afraid of that all along."

Trish tried to say something but Pastor Mort put a hand on her shoulder. "Let her cry it out," he whispered.

"Sometimes I get so angry at God—why is He doing this to me? And then I feel terrible. I know worry is a sin. I should—I have to—trust more."

Trish continued to rub and pat her mother's back. She looked up at her father. He buried his cheek in Marge's hair and held her tight to his chest.

God, help us, Trish pleaded.

It seemed her mother would cry forever. At times she was almost incoherent, muttering and sobbing as if her heart would break. Hal continued to hold her. Trish clung to his arm as she rubbed her mother's back, David on the other side, doing the same. Finally she fell silent, shuddering every once in a while.

Then Marge lifted her head from Hal's shoulder and took a deep breath. Hal dug a handkerchief out of his pocket, wiped her eyes and cheeks. She appeared to be past the deep grief she experienced at reliving the incident. "God, forgive me for what I have done to my family," Marge said. She kissed both David and Trish, then Hal.

"He does," replied Pastor Mort. "You know He does. And He'll help you put this behind you."

"I'll take you home." Hal wrapped both arms around his wife and hugged her close. "Unless there's more, Pastor?" The two men exchanged looks.

"No. We'll talk again on Monday, Marge, if you'd like." She nodded. "Good then. God bless you all." He hugged each of them in turn. "Remember, if you need me, all you have to do is call."

"I know." Hal shook the pastor's hand again. "Thank you."

Trish felt like a puppet with all the strings cut. She walked back to the car with her family and slumped in the back seat. *Now what will happen?* She rubbed her eyes with her fingers. After taking a deep breath, she glanced at her watch. The first race of the day was less than an hour away.

David leaned on the open car door and announced, "I've gotta get down to the stalls. Mom, you okay?"

Marge nodded. "I will be. You and Trish go ahead.

We'll go on home." She leaned back against the seat, closed her eyes, and reached back to squeeze Trish's hand. "You'll be okay—after all this, I mean?"

Trish lifted her mother's hand to her cheek. "Yes, Mom." She grabbed her sports bag and slid from the car. "I've missed you so." She whirled away before the tears could overwhelm her again.

"See you later." David back-pedaled as he talked, then turned and caught up with Trish. He put his arm around her shoulders. "You *really* all right? I mean, you'll be able to get beyond this and ride your mount?"

Trish nodded. "I feel like—like maybe there's hope now."

"Well, if I *never* go through something like that again, it'll be too soon."

"I know." Trish turned and watched as their family car was lost in the incoming vehicles. She shrugged her shoulders up to her ears and relaxed them. "See ya in the fifth." She turned left at the gate into the track, and David loped across the infield to the backside.

Trish was mounted on the favorite in the first race. Robert Diego's sorrel mare nickered when she saw Trish.

"I think you have a friend here." He shifted so Trish had room to stroke the mare's head and murmur sweet promises in the twitching ears.

"I like her too," Trish smiled back. "And today we're due for a win, aren't we?" She scratched the mare's cheek and up behind her ears.

"Two out of three would be a good number, no?" Diego boosted Trish into the saddle.

"Yes." Trish settled into the seat and gathered her reins. "See you in the winner's circle."

The sun had broken through the cloud cover to turn

the horse hides into dazzling colors. From the echoing bugle of the parade to post until the gates shut behind them, Trish knew there was no place on earth she'd rather be.

They broke clean at the shot and came off the pack by the end of the first turn. Trish sang to her mount, holding her steady about a half length ahead of the second place. She heard the cries of the jockeys and the grunts of the straining horses. When the other horse drew even with her stirrups, she loosened the reins. The mare settled lower, lengthening her stride. They pounded into the far turn, a two-horse race with the others trailing.

The other jockey went for his whip with a furlong to go. Trish leaned forward even more. "Go for it, you beauty. Come on. Now!" The mare turned it on and drove across the finish line three lengths ahead.

"I knew you could do it. And this was a nice fat purse too. You earned your feed for another year." She cantered on around the track, then dismounted at the winner's circle.

"An excellent ride." Diego shook her hand.

"I hate to say I told you so . . ." Trish grinned up at him.

"You're welcome to say that anytime."

They positioned themselves for the camera and Bob held the trophy aloft. The mare sniffed the silver bowl just as the cameras flashed.

"That oughta be a good one." Trish waved as she headed for the dressing room.

The next race didn't go as well, but with the quality of the horse Trish felt a place was pretty good. So did the owner, a man Trish hadn't ridden for before. She and the trainer exchanged smiles as the owner's wife stepped close enough to get sprayed by dirt when the horse shook.

In her next race John Anderson stood with David in the saddling paddock with his gelding Final Contender. "Good to see you, Trish." He shook her hand. "I'm sorry to miss your dad, but I know you two know this old boy better than anyone else. Just remember, I insist you use the whip if he needs it." David boosted Trish up and handed her a whip. He hid his wink in the horse's mane and backed the sorrel gelding out of the stall. They all knew how much Trish hated to use a whip, but this old boy seemed to need encouragement. He liked to run with the pack; winning wasn't on his list of priorities.

"We're gonna turn this into one of your priorities," Trish muttered at the flickering ears. "You and I both know you can run better than you've let anyone else guess."

Trish almost waited too long. Contender ran neck and neck with another horse, letting the leader pull away. "Too bad," Trish hollered as she brought the whip down on his shoulder—twice. A spurt of speed brought them up with the leader coming out of the turn. With a furlong to go, Trish whapped him again. Now the race was on. They thundered down the stretch, whisker to whisker.

The other jockey struck his horse again and just the thwap of it sent Contender surging ahead—to win by a nose.

"Well, that's the first time I'll have to thank another jockey for making my horse run faster," Trish commented to John Anderson when she slid to the ground.

"What happened?"

"This old boy didn't want to be hit again, so when

the other jockey went to the whip, we ran faster." She wiped sand out of her eyes. "Wish he didn't mind being behind. It gets mighty dirty that way." She patted the gelding's muddy face. "Thanks old boy. We done good."

Trish whistled her way across the infield after changing clothes.

"You sound mighty happy," Brad said as Trish dropped into a chair in their tack room.

"Good day. Fattened up my bank account some and had fun doing it. David still at the testing barn?"

"Yeah, should be here any minute. You hungry?"

"Starved."

"Good, let's hit the cook shack. I'll buy."

"No, I'll buy. We'll celebrate two out of three."

By the time they returned, David had Contender all rinsed off and was scraping him down. Brad took over the job while Trish handed David a ham sandwich and a can of soda.

"Thanks. To what do I owe this generosity?" David took a big bite out of one half.

"My wins." Trish sipped her Diet Coke. She poured some in her hand for Final Contender to lick. "I just feel so-o-o good." She handed Brad the sheet to throw over the steaming horse. "Here, I'll walk him. Then we can load and go home."

Hal lay dozing in his recliner when Trish and David walked into the house after finishing the chores. With only the gelding, Spitfire, and the foals to care for, chores didn't take long.

Trish's mind flew back to the months when Hal had been too weak to do much more than lie in his recliner. But his smile chased the fears back into hiding, even though she knew he was scheduled for another chemotherapy treatment on Monday.

"Where's Mom?" Trish asked.

"Sleeping."

"Is she. . . ?"

"No, no," Hal shook his head. "She's just resting. This has been a terribly exhausting day. But she put the roast in the oven before her nap, said we'd eat about six-thirty."

Trish felt the sigh reach all the way down to her toes. *What a relief*. She plunked down on the sofa and stretched her hands over her head.

"Well, how did you do?" Hal asked.

"Two wins and a place." She went on to tell her dad the story of Contender and the whips. They were laughing together when Marge yawned her way into the room.

The entire evening felt like evenings should feel, as far as Trish was concerned. No more mention was made of the morning at the track.

Until Sunday night. Trish knew her mother had a hard time during church, but she also knew if she let down, she'd have been sniffling too. She'd only had a place and a show at the track, but winning all the time didn't carry quite the urgency it did before the accident. Still, with the horses she'd ridden, those paying positions had been nothing to be ashamed of.

"Did you see this?" Hal asked when Trish walked in the door after chores. He handed Trish the sports section from *The Oregonian*, Portland's major newspaper.

A colored picture of her and Spitfire driving for the finish line covered most of the top half of the page. The headline read, "Can This Girl and Her Horse Win the Derby?" Trish grinned at her father over the top of the paper and then read through the article. Most of it seemed pretty accurate.

"They think just because no other woman has won the Derby, we don't have a chance."

"You're going to hear that a lot."

"But most of it depends on Spitfire. He does the running." Trish shook her head and finished the article. "They don't give him too much of a chance, do they?"

"You know Seattle Slew was a shocker because he came from the Pacific Northwest. The racing world doesn't think we have too much going out here."

"Humph." Trish snorted her opinion. She went back to reading the article—again. "At least they mention that Spitfire is a son of Seattle Slew. You'd think that would carry *some* weight. And how about the way he won the Santa Anita Derby? What's the matter with the jerk that wrote this?" She looked for the byline at the top of the article.

"Ken Davis is known as the best sportswriter in the area."

"He's a jerk."

"He's said plenty of good things about you in the past."

"Half a jerk, anyway." Trish grinned at her father.

"You better get used to it, Tee. You're going to hear, read, and see all kinds of stuff in the weeks ahead. Remember what they say, you're in trouble when you begin to believe your own press." Hal reached for her hand to pull him up from his chair. "Let's eat."

The family gathered for their weekly meeting after stuffing themselves with a fine meal of pork chops, potatoes and gravy. Marge's apple crisp added the final touch.

"Sure beats mine and Dad's cooking." Trish rubbed her stomach as she leaned back in her chair.

"You ain't just a kiddin'," David affirmed.

"Thanks a lot." Trish tossed her napkin at him. "I didn't see you in the kitchen, buddy."

Marge steepled her fingers together under her chin. "Thank you all for what you did for me and for all of us during the last several days. Trish, the eagle meant a lot to me, even if I didn't say so. And all the times each of you tried to get me to talk." A tear ran down one cheek, and she wiped it away. "Please forgive me."

Hal handed her a tissue. And then one to Trish. He and David got by without—just barely.

What about the Derby? Trish wanted to ask, but she bit her tongue and kept silent. Just having her family all together was enough for today.

CHAPTER 7

"I think you should go," Marge said quietly the next morning.

Trish darted a look at her father. He had that deep, considering look on his face. She wanted him to hurry and say "Yes, we're going to the Derby" so she could finish getting ready for school.

"How was Spitfire?" He turned to look at Trish.

"Rarin' to go. You said we might gallop tonight."

"Um-mm. We'll talk more after we see how that goes. Come on, Marge. Let's drop Trish off at school on the way in to the hospital."

Trish's good humor thumped back to earth. What kind of shape would her father be in when she got home? Would he be vomiting and weak again? If only he could wait for a treatment until after the Derby. Better yet, if only he never had to have another treatment. But she knew that was impossible. Since the cancer was receding, they didn't dare play around with the schedule the doctor had set up.

"No decision yet," Trish answered Rhonda's question as they stuffed books into their lockers.

"But at least your mom is better. Man, I was beginning to *worry*." Rhonda slung her purse strap over her shoulder.

"Don't even say that word." Trish slammed her locker door shut. "Let's eat before the food's all gone."

Brad joined them at their table a few minutes later. "You won't believe this." He shook his head as he tucked his long legs under the table.

"What's up?" Rhonda spoke around a mouthful of tuna salad sandwich.

"I won a scholarship. Mrs. Olson just told me about it. My dad is gonna freak out."

The girls threw their arms around his neck and each one kissed him on the cheek.

"That's fantastic." Trish kissed him again. "You deserve every penny."

"For how much?" Rhonda was always practical.

"And where to?"

Shock stole over Brad's face. "I don't know. Guess I just tuned out at the word scholarship."

Trish turned when she felt a hand tap her shoulder.

"Hi, Trish, my name is Lisa Jones, and I write for the sports section of the *Falcon Flyer*."

Trish nodded.

"I'd like to interview you for next week's paper, if that would be all right?" The thin girl tucked a strand of long, dark hair behind her ear. "Do you have time?"

"Sure." Trish shrugged. "When?"

"Would right now be okay?"

At Trish's nod, Brad moved over one seat. "Here, we even have a spot for you."

Lisa smiled at him and sank down onto the seat as if afraid he might jerk it out from under her.

Trish answered the questions easily.

When had she started riding? How long had she been racing?

She really got into it when she started describing the thrill of winning and what she liked best about her sport. The words flowed so fast that Lisa asked her to slow down a couple of times. It was a relief though when the bell rang—it kept Lisa from asking about the accident.

Or at least that was what Trish was afraid the young reporter would ask. "Scared to death" wouldn't look too good in the paper, but it would have been an honest answer.

But she'd worked through the fear, hadn't she? Trish sent a thank you heavenward.

Trish and Rhonda were still laughing and teasing Brad about his memory lapse over the scholarship when Trish got out of the car at Runnin' On Farm.

"Why don't you come ride with me?" Trish stuck her head back in the open window. "I'll be galloping Spitfire."

"Okay. Give me half an hour," Rhonda replied.

"What about me?" Brad assumed his soulful look.

"You know David'll find something for you to do."

"Great. I need the money."

"It's up to you." Trish waved as Brad pulled away. Caesar shoved his cold nose into Trish's hand. She scratched the top of his head, then jogged up the walk to the front door. Late-blooming red tulips filled two large pots on the sides of the concrete step. She hesitated before turning the brass doorknob. Both cars were in the drive, so she knew her parents were back.

Chicken, her nagging voice whispered. *Waiting isn't going to change anything.*

"I know." She stooped down to give Caesar a big hug. His tongue flicked her nose before she could pull back. "Still the fastest tongue in the west, aren't you, old boy?"

To prove her point, he caught her chin the next time.

Trish straightened up. "Just what I need, a clean face."

Caesar's feathery tail thumped his answer.

Trish opened the door and stepped into an empty living room, then the kitchen. Nope, no one in there, either. She stopped at the door to her parents' room. It stood ajar, and she peeked in. A deep breath didn't help the fluttering in her stomach.

Hal lay on his back in the dimness, one hand across his forehead. A large bowl sat on a chair by the bed.

When he didn't move, Trish turned to leave.

His voice, raspy but stronger than usual, stopped her. "I'll be okay by morning, Tee. Tell me how Spitfire's gallop goes."

"I will. Where's Mom?"

Hal started to answer but instead had to roll to the side and grab the yellow bowl. The sound of his gagging and spitting followed Trish down the hall.

Trish stopped in surprise when she entered her bedroom. Her mother lay soundly sleeping in Trish's bed. Trish tried to set her book bag down quietly, but Marge's eyes blinked open at the faint rustle.

She yawned and stretched her arms above her head. "Hi. Thanks for your bed. I didn't want to bother your dad, and the sun shining in your window was so inviting." She yawned again.

"You feeling okay?" Trish sank down on the edge of the bed and turned to face her mother.

"Just needed a nap. I think all that lying around zapped my strength." She sat up and scooted her back against the pillows. "How was school?"

"I got interviewed for the school paper." Trish leaned

over to unlace her tennis shoes. "Oh!" She jerked up-right. "Brad got a scholarship. And he forgot to ask for how much."

"Where to?"

"He didn't ask that either. Said he zoned out in shock at the word scholarship."

Marge laughed, then swung her legs over the edge of the bed. "Well, I'd better go bake that boy some cookies. He's coming over?" At Trish's nod, Marge stood and stretched again. "Chocolate chip, I suppose."

Trish heard her mother open the door and check on Hal, then continue into the kitchen.

Trish had no trouble giving thanks to God as one of the cards on her wall admonished.

Spitfire wanted to race when Trish trotted him out on the track a while later. Old Dan'l even crow-hopped a couple of times to give Rhonda a bit of a thrill. Neither horse was happy with the slow jog of the first lap.

"Knock it off," Trish ordered when the black colt lunged forward a couple of times. "Whaddya think you are, a charger?"

Spitfire shook his head, spraying gobs of lather from around the bit. One hit Rhonda in the face.

"Thanks a million," she said around her giggles. She wiped the sticky stuff onto Dan'l's shoulder.

"Dad says slow gallop once around and then jog again." Trish eased up on the reins but had to pull Spit-fire back down as he argued for a full-fledged race. Trish didn't dare let her mind wander for even an instant. It would be too easy for him to strain that knee again, and then it would be all over.

"Let's walk a loop," Trish said when they finished their jog. "Then we won't have to cool 'em out." She slid to the ground and started leading the colt around the track. Spitfire rubbed his sweaty forehead on her shoulder, nearly sending her flying. "Careful, you goof." She held the reins more tightly under his chin. By the time they finished the circuit, Spitfire had his head over her shoulder, right in his favorite place.

"Hard to believe he's a Derby contender when you see him like that," Rhonda said. "He looks more like a kid's pony right now."

"Yeah, let's just hope he gets a chance to run it."

After the chores were finished, the four teens took their cookies and milk out onto the deck. Marge brought a full plate to pass around again and joined them. Brad became the brunt of their teasing this time.

Trish felt as though she were standing off to the side watching what was going on. This happy scene had played out many times before in the years they'd all been growing up. You just never knew who would get teased the most and at what time. The only one missing was Trish's father. Caesar sat at her feet, eyes pleading for another piece of cookie. She tossed a chunk in the air and the collie caught it with a snap.

They didn't discuss the coming race until Tuesday evening. Trish felt as if she'd been walking on pins all day. They were scheduled to ship Spitfire in only two days.

"I've already given my opinion," Marge said at their family meeting around the dining room table. "I think you should go."

"Are you sure?" Hal clasped her hand between both of his.

"All that we've been through this past week, the talks with Pastor . . ." She paused and raised their clasped hands to her cheek. "I've realized I can't go on like I have been. I know I'm a worrier by nature—my mother was too, remember?"

Hal nodded.

"But I've got to turn it over to God. He says He can handle anything, so somehow He's going to teach me not to get myself sick worrying. He can take better care of you than I can." Tears glimmered in her hazel eyes. "So, I say go." Her voice dropped on the last word. She took a deep breath. "Besides that, I wrote to Mother, telling her they could meet you in Louisville to watch the race. That's not too far from Florida, even though Daddy hasn't been feeling well."

Trish felt hope leap in her chest. She stared from her father to her mother. "Do you think they'll come?"

"Who knows." Marge just shook her head.

Hal smoothed the hair back from his wife's cheek. "Well, that certainly puts a new slant on things. What do you say, David?"

"Mom and I'll handle things here. You go. Who knows if we'll ever have a Derby-quality horse again."

"And you, Trish? I know it's a waste of time to ask." His smile caused the dimple to show in his right cheek.

"Well, I don't want Mom to be sick again."

"I won't be."

"And you and David'll come for the race?"

Marge flinched, as if she'd been struck. "I—I don't know." Tension weighted the silence.

Hal cleared his throat. "That's not a decision that has to be made right now. We'll talk about that later."

Trish noticed the relief that caused her mother's shoulders to sag. So it really wasn't over yet. She swallowed the lump in her throat. "Kentucky, look out. We're on our way."

82

"David, I packed a lot of the tack today." Hal picked up as if there hadn't been a stress point in the conversation. "We'll load the pickup tomorrow, then let Trish work some of Spitfire's kinks out Thursday morning early. After that he should be easy to load. Our flight's scheduled for 1:30, so we should leave here about ten."

Trish tried to listen to the plans, but a new song played like a brass band marching through her head. *We're going. We're going. We're going to Kentucky. We're going. We're going.* The beat continued. She bounced a little bounce on her chair, then gripped the seat with both hands. Maybe she and the chair would just fly up out the roof.

"Thanks, Mom," she whispered as she hugged her mother good-night.

"You get right to sleep now. No Derby daydreaming." Marge hugged her daughter back.

Trish grinned at the words. "What? No homework first?"

A tiny frown lighted between Marge's eyebrows. "You're not behind, are. . . ?" Marge caught herself. She swatted Trish on the behind as Trish tried to dodge away. "Good-night, Tricia Marie Evanston."

Trish leaned over and hugged Hal, who was seated in his recliner. "Maybe I should stay home on Thursday and help load him."

"No, you're going to be missing too much school as it is. We'll be just fine. Now get to bed."

Trish didn't think she'd ever be able to fall asleep that night. She read each of her verses, then snuggled down under the covers. She never even got into the "pleases" in her prayer, there were so many "thank you's."

She'd expected Wednesday to drag by, but thanks to

a pop quiz in history and an in-class paper in English, the day flew by. Trish and Spitfire enjoyed a good gallop, and there was even time to work with Miss Tee for a while. The little filly still hesitated at leaving her dam, but once away she pranced along on the lead as if she'd never dug in her tiny hooves and almost landed on her rump due to a bad case of stubbornness.

"Have you started packing, Trish?" Marge asked at the dinner table.

"No, I don't go till Saturday."

"Never hurts to start early. You'll be racing Thursday and Friday, won't you?"

Trish nodded. Her mouth was too full to talk.

"I've got all your things ready." Marge smiled at Hal. "You just need to add your shaving gear in the morning."

"Bless you." Hal squeezed her fingers.

"And I put your tickets, maps, and reservations in your briefcase. The camera too."

"I wish you were coming with Trish," Hal said. "One of these days we're going to have to take a vacation. Maybe next year we can hire someone to manage here and we can all go to Santa Anita, or wherever."

"Let's think about *wherever*. I'd love to do something *not* associated with horse racing for a change." Marge's tone was wistful, as if she were reluctant to share *her* dream.

"You're right." Hal nodded.

You need to think of others' interests once in a while, Trish's little nagging voice punched her guilt button. *Not everyone wants to talk horses all the time.*

Trish felt a sigh of resignation creep over her unbidden.

"We'll be there for the race," David assured them

while reaching for his mother's hand. "Maybe we'll have time for some sightseeing. I'd like to visit Claiborne Farms and see their veterinary setup."

"You giving up on dogs and cats?" Trish looked at him in surprise. David had always talked about a small animal veterinary practice after he graduated from school.

"No, not really. Every vet has those. But maybe I should think of an equine specialty. I've sure gotten plenty of practice around here."

"And you've done an excellent job," Hal said. "You seem to have a sixth sense for what's ailing a horse like Trish does for riding. Maybe you should think about Tucson. Their equine research program is outstanding."

Besides the guilt that continued to nag her, Trish had two more things to think about when she went to bed. At least when David had been at Washington State University, they'd been able to go visit him. Arizona was a long way away.

Her thought switched to the scene at the table. Her grandparents had been invited to see her race. When they'd visited last summer, her grandmother hadn't been excited about Trish riding the thoroughbreds. In fact, she worried more than her daughter. Was worrying an inherited disease?

And was it really fair to ask so much of her mother? It was true that racing was the main topic of conversation in their home. *Why can't she love horses as much as Dad and I do?—or at least like them*?

It isn't the horses, her inner voice reminded her, *it's your riding—in races.*

"Thanks a bunch!" Trish took a deep breath, held it to the count of ten and let it all out. Her shoulders and rib cage seemed to melt into the mattress.

Light from the mercury yardlight showed her half-full suitcase on the chair. In the morning she'd ride Spitfire for the last time before Kentucky. *Please God, make everything go all right tomorrow* was her last conscious thought.

Spitfire was ready to play when she got down to the barn in the morning. He snatched her riding gloves out of her back pocket when she bent over to pick his front hoof, and tossed them in the corner.

"Whaddya think you're doing?" Trish scolded him.

Spitfire rolled his eyes and gave her a nudge when she bent over to pick up her scattered gloves. She caught herself before she went sprawling in the straw.

"Da-v-i-d." Trish called in the reserves.

"What's wrong?" David leaned over the stall door.

"Just hold on to his head, okay? He thinks he's Gatesby today."

"Or a clown in the circus?"

"Take your pick." Trish looked down at the tool in her hand. "Better yet, here. *You* pick and I'll hold."

They quickly had the colt cleaned and saddled. Trish waved as they trotted off to the track. Spitfire spooked at a gopher mound and shied when a bird flew up. He snorted and pranced, nostrils flaring red-pink as he tugged at the bit.

"You might as well give up," Trish told him. "You're not running today, just jog and loosen up." He danced sideways, reaching, pleading for more slack.

Each time he tugged, Trish pulled him down to a walk again. "See, I warned you." He shook his head. The next time she loosened the reins, he jogged peacefully all the way around the track and back to the barn. Mist had dampened both his hide and Trish's face. She could see steam rising from her horse when she slid to the ground.

"You better hustle or you'll be late for school," David greeted her.

"I think I should stay home until we get him on the plane."

"Dad said school."

Trish groaned but gave Spitfire one last hug before she raced for the house. Caesar beat her by one leap onto the deck.

"I'm hurrying." Trish correctly interpreted the look Marge gave her.

She slid into her seat at school just as the final bell rang.

"That was close," Rhonda whispered from across the aisle. "Thought maybe you'd decided to go along."

"Don't I wish." Trish opened her book.

"Put your books away and take out paper." The teacher turned to begin writing on the board. "This quiz will count for 25 points."

The class groaned, Trish adding her share.

She'd just started the last question when an announcement came over the intercom. "Will Tricia Evanston please report to the office."

Trish and Rhonda stared at each other.

"Don't panic," Rhonda ordered.

"Yeah." Trish grabbed her books and dashed out the door.

"Your mother will be here to pick you up. There's an emergency at home." The secretary looked sympathetic as she gave Trish the message.

CHAPTER 8

Trish flew out the door. She jerked open the car door before Marge brought the vehicle to a full stop.

"Trish, don't panic. No one's hurt," Marge said as Trish bounded into the seat.

"Then what. . . ?"

Marge laid her hand on Trish's knee. Her quiet voice calmed her, the same way that Trish's voice quieted a nervous horse. "They're having trouble loading Spitfire, so instead of fighting with him Dad said to go get you."

Trish slumped in the seat. *They should have let me stay home with him in the first place,* she thought, but was wise enough not to say it aloud. Her stomach returned to its normal place, rather than remaining parked up in her throat. "Man." She shook her head. "That message scared me out of a year's growth."

"Sorry," Marge answered as she looked both ways before pulling out onto 117th Avenue. "I didn't mean for them to scare you, just have you at the door by the time I got there."

"When they call your name over the intercom, you die, no matter what." Trish fluffed her bangs with her fingers. "Everybody in school is gonna wonder what's wrong now."

"In our case, it's what you do right. And that's handle Spitfire."

Please make it that simple, Lord, Trish prayed all the way home.

She leaped from the car before it completely stopped beside the pickup by the stables.

"Where is he?"

"Easy, Tee." Hal came from behind the horse trailer. "We put him back in his stall. He's all right."

Trish took a deep, calming breath before she walked up to Spitfire's stall. He poked his head out the door just as she reached for the latch. A silent nicker tickled his nose. He wuffled in her face, then rubbed his forehead on her chest.

"You crazy animal," Trish crooned as she rubbed his ears and smoothed the coarse black forelock. "What'd you cause such a fuss about?" She adjusted the travel sheet that rode high on his neck.

"Well, let's get this over with." Hal stopped beside her. "You and David both take the leads, even though he looks calm as a kitten right now. I don't know what your magic is Trish, but it sure works."

"Just love." Trish kissed Spitfire on the nose.

The colt stepped out calmly when Trish swung open the stall door. He draped his head over her shoulder and only hesitated at the edge of the ramp. After a gentle tug on the rope, he followed Trish right into the trailer.

"Don't even say it," David growled as he slip-tied the lead rope.

"You mean, I told you so?" Trish hid her grin as she tied her rope. "I wouldn't dream of it." She patted Spitfire's shoulder and slipped out of the trailer.

Hal and David lifted the gate in place and threw home the bolts.

"I think you'd better go with us to the airport," Hal said. "Just in case. We're late now so let's get a hustle on."

"You be careful now," Marge said as she hugged Hal one more time. "And call me as soon as you get settled."

"I will. And I've plenty of help on call so you needn't worry."

"Easy for you to say," Marge muttered under her breath.

Hal hugged her again. "You're doing great." He climbed up into the cab. "Let's roll."

Trish felt as if she were in one of the old Westerns. Her dad was the wagonmaster with "Let's hit 'em up and roll 'em out," but that wasn't exactly what he said.

"Make something good for lunch," Trish called as she waved to her mother.

David poked her in the ribs with his elbow. "Smart aleck."

"You remember what school food is like. If I'm home, I take advantage of it." Trish settled herself between the broad shoulders of the two men. Good thing they had a large pickup.

The drive over the I–205 bridge to the airport passed with Hal giving them last minute instructions for the horses at home.

"I don't know why I'm telling you all this," he finally said. "You know what to do. And Trish, you won't have time for anything. Saturday'll be here soon." He turned the truck into a driveway marked Eagle Transport.

A guard stopped them for their names, then waved the truck through after giving Hal instructions for finding their plane. It was the only one on the concrete in front of the hangars. A ramp led up to a wide cargo door on the silver body of the aircraft. An emblem of a flying eagle adorned the vertical section of the tail.

Hal parked the trailer near the ramp and pulled his briefcase from behind the seat. "You two wait here until I get checked in. Don't let me forget my suitcases."

"Is he excited or what?" Trish turned to David with a serious look on her face.

David shook his head. They could hear Spitfire moving around in the trailer. A jet roared up into the sky from the east/west runway just beyond the loading area. They could hear the trailer creak in protest to Spitfire's shifting.

"You better get back there with him." David peeled out the door. "You know he doesn't like strange noises."

Spitfire whinnied when Trish opened the front door and ducked under the bar to stand beside him. At the roar of another jet under full thrust, he threw his head up as far as the ties permitted.

Trish sang her comfort songs to him, stroking the colt all the while. She rubbed his ears and neck, feeling the sweat popping out from his tension. Spitfire rubbed his head against her shoulder and shuddered when another plane took off.

"Keep up the good work, Tee," Hal said as he stuck his head in the door. "We'll get the tack boxes loaded first. How's he doing?"

"Better. Just like schooling at the track. Maybe we should have brought him here a few days ago and let him get used to the noise. Walked him through the process."

"Too late now. We'll be just a few minutes."

She could hear him giving orders to David and someone else. Spitfire flinched when the tack boxes screeched during the unloading. Another jet took off. This time the colt just shifted his feet. Trish checked the thick leg wraps that David or her father had secured on all four legs to keep the horse from injuring himself. The crimson and gold travel sheet covered Spitfire from behind his ears to his tail.

"You look good," she murmured to his drooping ears. He only jerked his head when another jet lifted off. "They sure send plenty of planes out of here."

"Okay, Trish." David stopped at the door before going to the rear to drop the ramp. "We're ready."

"This is it, fella." Trish jerked the loose end on her lead shank and freed the other. David slipped in on the other side as soon as the ramp was down. "Here." Trish handed him one of the ropes. "Okay, Spitfire, back up."

Once out on the concrete, Spitfire raised his head and looked around. David and Trish let him look, watching his ears and eyes for any sign of tension. When he relaxed, they started walking toward the plane ramp. Spitfire looked from side to side, observing the activity around him.

When Trish and David started up the padded ramp, he followed like a docile puppy. Until another jet, a huge one, thundered into the air not a hundred yards away. Spitfire reared. As he went up, Trish let the rope slip through her fingers, then leaped for his halter when he came down. His feet slipped.

Trish flinched at the pain in her leg where the colt's flailing legs had struck her. But she didn't let go and didn't stop talking to him.

When he tried to go up again, she clamped her hand over his nostrils.

"No!" Her order penetrated the black's fears. His

front feet stayed on the ground this time. They stood at the edge of the ramp, the horse and Trish both shaking, and David scolding the colt under his breath.

"That was close." Hal kept his voice low and soothing. "Walk him around a bit and let's try it again. He was fine until that plane took off."

Trish didn't have any spit to swallow. Her mouth felt like she'd been sucking on cotton balls. She nodded, and coaxed Spitfire to follow her.

When they approached the ramp again, Spitfire followed them up and into the dimness.

"Good fella," Trish encouraged him. "Just keep it up now until we get the stall up around you." They tied their ropes to one side of a padded wooden stall that was guy-wired in the center floor of the plane. Quickly, the airline crew bolted and wired the remaining three sides around the shivering colt.

Eyes rolling, nostrils flaring, Spitfire tossed his head when Trish started to leave the stall. His tail twitched and all four feet created their own staccato dance step.

Trish stepped back to his head and kept on rubbing, soothing him with her voice and hands.

"How close to packed is your suitcase?" Hal stroked Spitfire's neck under the soaking sheet.

"Why?"

"I don't think you better leave this stall. I've got a tranquilizer along but I hate to use it. You never know how he might react. So-o-o, the way I see it, we better take you along."

Trish rose on tiptoe to kiss her father's cheek. "What's Mom gonna say?"

"Probably plenty, but I don't know what else to do. David, unhitch the trailer so you can make better time.

I'll call home and make the arrangements. Trish, you just keep a lid on the kid here. I'll be back to help you as soon as I've made the call."

"Dad, you need to make a list of the things to tell Mom. Like, my silks are hanging in the closet, along with the hang-up clothes I planned to bring. My makeup's in the bathroom, shampoo and stuff. Oh, and my sports bag."

"We can buy things there if you need more," Hal looked up from his list. "David can pick up your books and lessons at school and ship them, plus whatever else you need from home."

"Is this gonna make Mom mad, or sick again?"

"No. It's only two days early. Maybe a shock, that's all. You forget, she's really been praying about her worrying, and besides, she's much better."

"I know." Trish chewed on her bottom lip.

"Anything else?"

Trish looked up to see her father smiling at her. She could feel the love shining from his eyes.

"No. I'm—we're fine."

Hal patted her shoulder and headed toward the door.

"Tell David to bring some carrots," Trish called to his retreating back.

Spitfire shuddered again as another jet began its journey. "What are you gonna do when that's us taking off?" Trish asked. "You won't just hear it, you'll feel it."

Spitfire draped his head over her shoulder. His sigh matched the one Trish felt squeeze past the cotton in her throat.

Two more planes had lifted into the sky before Hal returned. "All set." He handed Trish a soft brush. "See if you can brush him dry. I'll get a dry sheet as soon as we're airborne."

"What did Mom say?"

"That she loves you and she's praying for all of us."

"Did you tell her how Spitfire acted?"

Hal raised one eyebrow. "I'll hold him while you brush."

"We need to get this crate off the ground pretty quick." A man from the airline approached Hal. "How long till your son gets back?"

Just then Trish heard a truck door slam. David bounded up the ramp, clutching Trish's suitcase, plus Hal's garment bag from the back of the truck. Marge followed right behind him with Trish's garment bag and her sports bag.

"Mom!" Spitfire lifted his head when Trish raised her voice. "You came." Trish's grin lit the entire interior of the plane.

"You think I'd let you get away without a hug?" Marge reached over the stall and suited action to words.

Trish clung to her for a moment. "Thanks for getting all my stuff together. Good thing you told me to pack early."

Marge smiled. "You call me tonight if you need anything else. And I'm sure they have stores in Louisville, too—" She hugged her daughter again. "Just in case."

"Excuse me, folks," the airline representative interrupted. "The captain says he's behind schedule, so we need to get the doors closed."

"Behave yourself."

"You talking to me or the horse?" Trish raised her eyebrows at her brother.

"Both." David punched her shoulder. "See you at the Derby."

Trish hugged her mother again. "Please come," she

whispered. "It wouldn't be the same without all of us together."

"I know." Marge's hug bordered on the fierce side. "Take care of your dad."

Trish felt that familiar lump in her throat when she watched her parents say goodbye. It wasn't as if they wouldn't be together again soon. Why did she feel so close to crying? She wiped her cheek against Spitfire's mane.

As they closed the doors, Hal climbed over the stall. "Just in case you need another couple of hands."

Spitfire nosed Hal's pockets. "Smarty." Hal pulled out a carrot and broke it in chunks. Spitfire chewed the first piece as engine number one roared to life. He shifted front feet at the surge of number two. Head up, nostrils flaring, he ignored the carrot Hal offered as engine three thrust awake.

Trish pulled his head back down and rubbed his ears and cheek. Spitfire shuddered along with engine four.

"Easy, fella, easy." Both Trish and her father kept up the easy flow of words, all the while alert for any sudden moves on the colt's part.

The plane taxied forward, engines building as they turned onto a side runway and trundled down to the take-off point.

Spitfire shifted restlessly. His front feet beat their own tattoo in the deep straw.

The plane turned again. The engines crescendoed and the plane shuddered as it built speed.

Spitfire shook. His muscles twitched and his eyes rolled white. But he stood firm under Trish's loving hands.

With a final roar, the plane lifted off the concrete and

thrust itself into the sky. Trish braced against the slant. Spitfire nickered and threw his head up as far as the ropes allowed.

"Easy, come on, it's almost over." Trish breathed a sigh of relief when she felt the plane level out. She yawned to release the pressure in her ears and looked over at her father. His look of I'm-sure-glad-that's-over made her grin.

Spitfire took another piece of carrot.

"You're glad too, aren'tcha fella?" Trish whispered in his ear. She smoothed his forelock, grateful she could unclamp her hand from the halter. She flexed her fingers.

"I'll get some hay and water in here for him." Hal climbed over the wall. "And how about something to drink for you, too?"

"I could use that." Trish yawned again. Her left ear popped this time. She frowned. "I think I liked the noise level better when I couldn't hear."

Hal chuckled as he rummaged in their supplies. He handed a dry sheet over the wall after the drinks. "You want some help changing that?"

Trish just shook her head. There was plenty of room to move around in the stall so who was he kidding? She'd been grooming horses since she was ten. She stripped off the damp sheet and brushed the now-weary horse down again. With the dry sheet buckled on, she stepped back to view her handiwork.

When Spitfire finally cocked one rear foot and dozed off, Trish sank down in the corner. She didn't dare leave the stall in case something happened, but sitting sure beat standing. She didn't realize she'd dozed off until she heard the engines change and the plane begin its descent into the Louisville airport.

Spitfire flinched when the wheels touched down, but other than that he remained quiet. Even when the men broke down the stall around him, he just watched, his head draped over Trish's shoulder.

Hal took the other lead rope just in case, but Spitfire walked off the plane like he'd been traveling in such style all his life. He walked right into the horse van waiting for them. Trish unsnapped the ropes so Spitfire could inspect his new quarters. After a quick hug, she shut the door and leaped to the ground.

"How about dropping me off to pick up my rental car and then I'll follow you to the track?" Hal asked the van driver.

"Sure." White teeth flashed as a smile split the man's fudge-colored face. "That's a ma-aghty fine-lookin' colt you have there. Been hearin' some about him."

"Fred, this is my daughter, Tricia." Hal laid a hand on her shoulder. "Trish, Mr. Robertson."

Trish extended her hand as she'd been taught. Her fingers disappeared in the width of the man's hand.

"Just call me Fred." He tipped his hat after releasing the handshake. "You the young miss they all in a sweat about? Say you and that black colt maaght make racin' history."

Trish grinned back. "Winning the Derby will be kinda exciting."

She heard little nagger snort. *Kinda exciting?*

The three of them climbed up in the high cab. Trish felt the truck rock as Spitfire continued his inspection. She listened as Fred and her father talked about the area and what had gone on so far at the track. Nomatterwhat, the sorrel favorite they'd beaten at Santa Anita had arrived the weekend before. Dun Rovin', a Kentucky-bred colt that took the honors at Gulf Stream in Florida, had arrived on Wednesday. Equinox, the current favorite, was shipping in on Saturday.

Trish felt two shivers chase each other up and back down her spine. She was *really* in Kentucky. It wasn't just a dream or a wish any longer. The race was two weeks from Saturday, sixteen days away. Sixteen days of butterflies.

"Trish, you ride with Fred in case you're needed, okay?" Hal hesitated before shutting the truck door. At Trish's nod, he slammed the door and waved.

"This your first trip here?" Fred turned off the engine.

"Uh—huh. My first racing season too. Spitfire's the first colt we've had this good. Dad's been training for a long time, but only in the Northwest."

"And this colt brought you into the big time." Fred leaned back against the door. "Y'all must be maaghty proud."

"You been hauling horses long?"

"Seems like all my life. This way ah get to be part of the business."

"Tell me about some of the horses you've seen."

"Why, I hauled Secretariat himself. Now that horse, he knew he was king." Fred chuckled. "Course ah was a bit younger then. Summer Squall, now he looked maaghty good, too. You seen Seattle Slew, haven't you?"

"No, but he's Spitfire's sire."

Fred waved back when Hal walked from the car rental building to the burgundy four-door car. Fred turned the key and the engine surged to life. He hummed a little under his breath as he pulled out onto the road. "Now, ah remember when . . ." His stories kept Trish enthralled all the way to the freeway and over the surface streets following the signs to Churchill Downs. Huge trees shaded the houses along Central Avenue. Traffic increased as they neared the track.

"Last race about done," Fred commented. "You watch ahead, we're almost there."

Trish checked her side mirror to make sure her father was still behind them. Horse trucks and trailers filled a lot on their right and concrete-block stables lined the chain-link fence on their left.

Fred shifted down and signaled his turn. They had arrived. The guard at the gate waved them through. Fred eased the truck down the main road running between stables.

Trish could see the track off to her right, the triple cupolas that marked the famed racetrack visible on the roof of the grandstand.

It seemed like they drove forever. Trish tried to see everything at once as Fred pointed out the steward's office, the media building, the first-aid station and finally barn 41. This barn at the back of the backside housed all the Derby contenders. With a green roof, white trim, and concrete block walls, the stable seemed to stretch out a mile. Everything looked freshly painted, even to the green and white sawhorses that marked parking restrictions.

Fred laughed softly. His contagious chuckle brought a grin to Trish's face, too.

"Well—" Trish took a deep breath and let it out. "Thanks for such a great ride." She unbuckled her seat belt. The truck shifted as Spitfire moved around. He nickered.

"Y'all take care now, you hear?" Fred opened his door. "And I'll be a watchin' you, 'specially in that winner's circle."

"Thanks." Trish stepped down and went around the truck to unload. Two men already had their microphones in front of her father's face, asking him questions. Trish helped Fred let down the ramp.

Spitfire whinnied, a shrill announcement that he had arrived. Horses down the lines answered.

"He's tellin' 'em, Look out. Ah'm here." Fred chuckled again and shook his head. "That boy not gonna take nothin' from nobody."

"Back up," Trish ordered when she opened the door. Spitfire nuzzled her shoulder and did as he was told. His flaring nostrils showed that he knew this was a strange place and he was ready to check it out. "Just take it easy now," she talked as she snapped the two shanks on his halter, slipping one chain section over his nose in case he got rowdy.

Spitfire posed in the doorway. Head high, ears pricked forward, he surveyed his kingdom. He answered another whinny from a stabled horse, then blew in Trish's face and followed her down the ramp.

"Are you Tricia Evanston?" a voice called.

CHAPTER 9

Spitfire danced in a circle around Trish, effectively scattering the three people who waited. "Behave yourself now," she ordered sternly. "Sorry, but he's had a long day."

"We're in stall five, halfway down." Hal checked the paper in his hand. "Let's get the sheet off him, then you can walk him and get the kinks out while I get us settled."

"If you've got as many kinks as I do, we're in deep trouble," Trish said as she led Spitfire after her father. The horse rubbed his forehead on her shoulder. He seemed to be walking on tiptoe as he paraded after her, eyes and ears checking out everything around him.

The colt shook all over like a wet dog when Hal pulled off the crimson and gold sheet and folded it to air over the open halfwall that fronted the stalls. Hard-packed dirt aisles and shade from the overhanging roof kept the interior cooler than outside.

"Come on, fella." Trish didn't need to tug on his lead rope. As they left the building Spitfire raised his head and whinnied again. "Knock it off, you want to break my eardrums?" Trish watched him for any nervousness but Spitfire seemed calm. He was just letting everyone know he was there. They strolled up and down the wide areas between barns. Some were gravel, some deep sand. Some stables were decorated with hanging flower baskets, others displayed signs. Bandages, blankets, sheets, all the gear of any track hung drying on the lines strung between the posts on the half-walls.

The sun was setting behind the barns when Trish and Spitfire found their way back. Hal had set up their room at the end of the barn; deep straw filled the stall, with a hay net hanging in a corner. Spitfire walked to the bucket and took a deep drink. While he buried his nose in the grain pan, Hal stroked down the colt's legs, checking for any heat or swelling.

"We'll leave the wraps on tonight in case he gets restless, but I think he's ready for a good night's sleep." He patted the horse's shoulder. "I know I am."

"You know how to get where we're going?" Trish asked as she hooked the web gate over the stall entrance.

"Sure." Hal grinned at her questioning look. He patted his pocket. "I have a map."

"Can we eat soon? I'm starved." Trish looked around their office for her suitcases. "Where's my stuff?"

"In the car. Fred helped me get everything moved around."

"I didn't get to tell him goodbye. He was such a neat man."

"He said he'd see us again before the race. He thought you were all right too." Hal put an arm around her shoulder. "Let's hit the road."

Birds twittered their night songs in the stately oak trees that shaded the backside track entrance. A horse whinnied off to their left and another answered. Somebody picked a guitar, the simple tune floating on the gentle breeze. It was a track settling down for the night.

It could be any track, but it wasn't. They were at *Church-ill Downs*. Trish gave a little skip as she rounded their car.

Hal handed her the map when they were inside. "Here, you navigate." He pointed to the circular mark indicating the racetrack, and then pointed out the streets that led to the hotel. "It's right off the freeway, back the way we came in, so we shouldn't have any trouble."

Trish glanced through the brochure. "Jacuzzis in each suite? All right!"

"Just pay attention to where we're going," Hal teased her. "We'll think about hot tubs later." He waved at the guard at the gate and turned right. "You want to eat before we check in, or wait and have dinner at the hotel?"

"Let's eat now."

Trish sighed as she climbed back into the car after dinner. "Funny, I knew about southern accents, but I feel like an idiot saying Huh? or Excuse me? all the time. I gotta listen up."

"It never seems like we have an accent, but we must," Hal said. "That waitress asked us right away where we were from."

"I never think of saying Washington *state*. Kinda forget there's another Washington." Trish glanced from her map to see where her father was turning. "Should be one more exit, and then ours."

Hal parked under the portico of the New Orleans-style building with wrought-iron trim.

"I think I'm gonna like it here." She gave her father the thumbs up sign.

"I *know* I'm gonna like it here," she repeated as she stared at the huge oval, rose-colored Jacuzzi tub in their bathroom. She almost needed a step-stool to get into it.

"Think it'll be okay?" Hal asked after tipping the bell-boy. "Good grief, that thing is almost as big as a swimming pool."

"And I'm getting in right away." Trish read the instructions on the wall. She picked up the little bottles nesting in a basket of tri-folded pink washcloths. "There's even bubblebath." She turned on the taps and adjusted the temperature. The bottle of blue gel she dumped in began to foam immediately. "Now I'll hang up my stuff. That thing'll take forever to fill."

A sitting room with a sofa hide-a-bed separated the two bedrooms of their suite. Horse pictures, both racing and fox hunting, decorated the walls. French doors opened onto a grilled balcony overlooking the central courtyard where glass-topped, wrought-iron tables awaited the breakfast buffet crowd.

Trish flopped on her back across the queen-size bed in her room. Even with her arms spread eagle she didn't touch the sides. She raised on her elbows and looked at herself in the mirror above a chest of drawers. She stuck out her tongue at the grinning face in the mirror, and got up to empty her suitcases into the drawers and closet. Her tub was not even half-full yet.

"Tell Mom hi for me," she said as she closed the bathroom door. "And tell her I'm soaking in this monstrous tub. Maybe that'll convince her to come."

Trish pinned her hair up on top of her head. The waterline was finally above the jets. The water churned to life with a turn of the dial on the wall. When she was ready to climb in, she rolled one towel to put behind her head, and sank into the hot, bubbling water up to her neck. Her toes just touched the opposite end. She flexed one foot over a jet and played with another with her hand. This was living!

By the time she forced herself to get out and get ready for bed, her father was already fast asleep. Trish thought about turning on the TV, but when a huge yawn stretched her entire jaw, she crawled into bed.

She screamed and screamed again but no sound came. She couldn't get enough air. The horse was dead. A jockey, too. Ambulance sirens. More screams. Something was holding her prisoner; she couldn't move. Why was her mother fading away?

"Trish, Trish, it's all right now. You're dreaming." Hal shook her gently. "Wake up, Tee."

Trish jerked upright. She sucked in a huge gulp of air. She shook her head and blinked her eyes. "Where's Mom?"

"At home. Trish, everything is okay. You had a bad nightmare."

"I sure did." Trish slumped against the pillows. "I thought those terrible dreams were all over. Dad, I was so scared. I thought I was dying—and Mom wouldn't talk to me—and . . ." She buried her face in her hands.

"And?"

"And I shouldn't be so scared. My Bible verse says, 'Fear not,' so if He's with me why am I so scared? And I keep thinking that if I didn't race, Mom wouldn't worry so much."

"And so you feel guilty, too." Hal smoothed her hair back from her forehead.

Trish nodded. She sniffed and reached for a tissue on the nightstand. "Yeah, it's like I have this little voice in my head that keeps yelling that everything's all my fault." She rubbed her temples with her fingers. "Sometimes I even get a headache from it all."

"Tee, I think you have a serious problem."

"I know."

"No, look at me." He tipped her chin up with a loving finger. "Your problem is—you're human, just like the rest of us."

"Da-a-d."

"No, I mean it. The fears and the guilt are all part of our humanity. And teenagers seem to attract guilt like a magnet. So do those who don't really understand God's grace."

"I know He takes care of my fears." Trish told her father about the time at the track. "I went on and rode that day. And it's been better ever since."

"That's wonderful."

"I know. But then the nightmare makes it all worse again."

"So you claim your verses again, confess your fears, your guilt, and go on. That's what it takes to build faith. Just like you stretch your muscles; they get sore but they also get stronger. Faith is really like a muscle. Use it or lose it."

"You make it sound so simple." Trish twisted her fingers in her lap.

"Remember the rest of the 'Be not afraid' verse?"

Trish nodded. "For I am with you."

"He never gives an order without a promise." Silence wrapped comfort around them. "Be right back." Hal returned in a few moments with the carved eagle and set it on her nightstand. "Just a reminder. For when *you* need those eagle's wings."

Trish threw her arms around his neck. "I love you."

Hal hugged her back. "And I love you. Good-night,

and good dreams this time." Trish nestled back down in the bed, and Hal pulled the covers up over her shoulder. Then he switched off the lamp.

The next thing she knew, her father was knocking at her door. "Time to get up. I'll be waiting for you downstairs by the buffet."

Trish stretched both arms above her head and then all the way to her toes. The nightmare seemed dim and far away, like most dreams do upon waking. She glanced at the eagle, spiraling where the air currents led. Her feet hit the floor running. What a great day to be alive.

Downstairs, she grabbed an apple, toast, and a strip of bacon. "I'm ready."

Spitfire was ready too when they got to the track— ready to eat. Trish measured his grain and refilled the water bucket. "There you go, enjoy." She patted his shoulder as she went by.

Shoulder to shoulder, she and Hal leaned on the track fence and watched the morning works already in progress. *I don't know anybody here*, Trish thought as she watched one rider argue with her horse. *At Santa Anita we weren't there long enough, but here . . .*" She shrugged. Maybe she'd get some sun and studying done this way. "Did you remind David to pick up my books? And assignments?"

"He did that yesterday afternoon. They'll be here Monday."

"Good—I think."

Hal nodded. "You'll have to work hard next week. Derby week'll keep us plenty busy."

Trish watched another horse breeze by. "Sure hope Mom comes. Do you think she will?"

"I keep praying. And I know she is, too." He checked

his watch. "Spitfire oughta be done by now. Let's get him out on the track."

Spitfire rubbed the grain stuck to his whiskers on Trish's cheek and blew some more in her hair.

"Thanks." She wiped off what she could. "Do you want to pick or brush?" She offered her father the choice. It seemed so strange to be working with him instead of David. The thought made her think of home again. Here she was, already missing her brother and mother. *Great!*

"I'll pick." Hal handed her the brush. He lifted a front hoof and bent to the task.

Trish hummed to herself as she brushed her way around the horse. Even in the dimness of the stall, Spitfire's coat shone with health and good care.

Her father leaned against the wall after he'd finished his job.

"You okay?" Trish paused in her brushing.

"Yeah. Just not used to bending over so much. You and David have spoiled me." Trish heard a slight wheeze when he talked.

"Here." She tossed him the brush. "I'll take off the bandages while you get the saddle."

"No, leave 'em on." He unhooked the web gate and left.

"He worries me sometimes," Trish confessed to Spitfire's twitching ears.

There you go again, worrying, her little nagger whispered. *See how easy it is?* Trish shook her head and rolled her eyes toward her eyebrows.

Spitfire stood quietly while she adjusted the saddle. He even dipped his head down for her to slip the headstall over his ears. Trish smoothed his forelock in place and took a deep breath. "Well, let's go, fella, your public awaits." She led him out the stall and turned right. The horse on the end, stall one, stuck his head over the gate and nickered. "Who's that?" Trish asked.

"Nancy's Request. He's owned by that singer down in Hollywood. Haven't heard much about him 'cause he might not run."

"Problems?" She waited for her father to give her a knee up.

"Some. Keeps coming up sore behind and they're not sure why." He boosted Trish aboard. "Now you take him slow and easy. Walk one to let him see everything, and then jog." He patted her knee.

"Tell *him* that." Trish stroked Spitfire's neck. She clucked him forward and Hal walked with them up to the entrance to the track. Then he continued on to the wooden bleachers set up for trainers and media people to watch the horses.

Trish let Spitfire stand watching the action. Other horses came and went. An exercise rider hit the dirt just past the gate and her horse galloped on around the track. She stood up and dusted herself off, disgust written all over her face. It took the red-jacketed assistants several tries to catch the runaway. The horse proved adept at dodging.

When Trish nudged Spitfire forward, he walked flat-footed out onto the track. They kept near the outside rail so as not to get in the way of those working faster. Trish felt like both she and Spitfire had swivels in their necks as they tried to see everything at once. The stands stretched from just past the first turn to the other. A turf track lay inside the dirt oval and its grass was as green as that on the infield. All the official tote boards sported a fresh coat of dark green paint, and the two-story hex-agonal building that centered the horseshoe-shaped winner's circle glistened white. Stairs inside led to the celebrity viewing area up above. Churchill Downs, lettered in gold, graced the base of the building. A bright red horseshoe of flowers set off the green turf around it. Just beyond that, gold knobs topped the two tall round posts with "CD" and "finish" lettered in gold.

"Impressive, huh, old boy?" Trish turned her head to see the rest of the floral plantings in neat rows of yellow, red, and orange. "You look that horseshoe over good, 'cause we want to be standing there when this is all over."

A horse galloped on by them, drawing her attention to the fountain that jetted a column of water ten feet in the air. "Awesome. Totally awesome."

After jogging their two laps, Trish rode back to their barn. She'd expected to meet her dad at the gate, but when she didn't see him they kept on walking. She found him leaning against the wall, struggling to breathe. The half-cleaned stall told her what he'd been doing.

"What's the matter with you?" she scolded. "You know better than to work in that dust." She planted both hands on her hips, still clasping the reins in one. "Just leave that and . . ."

"Yes, boss." Hal touched a finger to his cap. His sarcasm cut off her tirade.

"Sorry." Trish handed him the reins. "Why don't you walk him out and I'll . . ." She stopped again. Her father didn't need to do that much walking right now, either. *David, I need you.* "No. You put away the tack and I'll walk him. Then you can hold him while I clean. Okay?" She unbuckled the saddle and bridle while she talked, deliberately not looking her father in the eye. She knew how much he hated to admit any weakness.

She heard him coughing when she brought Spitfire back into the barn.

CHAPTER 10

"Dad? If you can hold him, I'll finish the stall."

Hal nodded. "The water is helping." He took another drink and, leaning against the block half-wall, held out his hand for the reins. Spitfire nosed the cup. When he started to nibble the rolled paper edge, Hal shook his head. "Not for you, old man. Yours is in the bucket."

Trish left the two of them discussing the water cup, and attacked the dirty straw. By the time she'd loaded and trundled out a couple of wheelbarrow loads, sweat was running down her neck.

When she started to load a straw bale on the barrow, a voice stopped her. "Why don't you let me do that?"

She turned to look into the bluest eyes she'd ever seen, except in the movies. He had curly red hair—not carrot, but deep auburn, and he was grinning at her. She couldn't resist grinning back.

"They call me Red but my name's Eric." He hefted the bale and dumped it in her barrow. "Another?"

"Yeah, thanks. I'm Tricia Evanston, Trish." Before she could pick up the handles, he had the wheelbarrow in motion. "You don't have to do this. I *can* manage."

"I know."

"Stall five." She kept pace with him.

"I know. You ride Spitfire and you're from Washing-

111

ton, as in, state of. This is your first time to Kentucky, and most people think the world will end if a girl should win the Derby."

"How . . ."

"I can read. They do teach us southern boys how to read before they let us up on horseback. But me, I was riding before I started reading." He lifted the bales out one at a time and dumped them in the stall.

Trish snapped her mouth closed. She looked at her father in time to catch a slow wink.

"Gotta go. See y'all later, maybe down at the Track Kitchen. Only one more mount this morning." He walked off whistling.

Hal took one look at Trish's face and started to laugh. Even a cough in the middle didn't make him quit chuckling.

"What's so funny?" Trish cut the baling wires with a pair of pliers, pulled out the wire and wrapped them together to throw away. Then she took a pitchfork and broke up the bale. Tossing the straw in the air to separate it sent clouds of dust billowing up. "Don't know what made him think he could do this stuff," she muttered as she worked. "There must be someone here we can hire to help."

"Kinda takes your breath away, doesn't he?"

"Who?" Trish pulled her leather gloves off and stuck them in her back pocket. She wiped her forehead with her sleeve. "Where'd you find that water?"

Hal pointed to a hose outside. "That jockey who helped you."

"Jockey? He was probably just an exercise boy." Trish downed a cup of water.

"Don't you know who he is?"

"Red, or Eric. That's all he said. I didn't *ask* him for help, you know." Spitfire rubbed his forehead against her shoulder, then lipped the cup. "Get away, your drink's in your stall." She pushed his nose away.

"Do you care who he is?"

"Not particularly. Right now I'd rather eat." She squatted down and started unwrapping the thick bandages Spitfire still wore. As she finished each one, she handed it to Hal, who hung it over the wire strung between the posts. When she finished that, she checked the stall. "Dust's down. He can go in." She led the colt into his stall and let him loose. "Be good now." One last pat on his rump, and she slipped out of the stall while he drank.

Trish picked up the bucket with brushes, scraper, and sponge to store in one of the wardrobe-size tack boxes. She added her pliers, gloves, and helmet, then glanced around to make sure nothing was left lying around. Her father had taught her well; loose gear meant lost gear.

In the car Hal leaned back against the headrest with his eyes closed. His breathing was shallow with an occasional wheeze. He handed Trish the keys. "You better drive, at least on the grounds here."

Trish adjusted the seat for her shorter legs and turned on the ignition. "Am I legal in this car?"

"Not really. Should have had you sign on the contract just in case." Hal opened his eyes. "I'll be okay after some hot coffee and food."

Trish found a place to park right in front of the brick building shaded by massive oak trees. Track Kitchen—the sign above the white double-wide doors read. White shutters at the windows, and white bricks outlining the flower beds and trees made it look more like a nice home than a cafeteria.

Trish headed for the restroom before getting in line for her food. One look in the mirror at her dirt-streaked face and she groaned. Great way to meet a new guy.

Thought you weren't interested, her little nagger chuckled teasingly.

"I'm not—I mean, I—" Trish stuffed the wet paper towel in the trash. She pulled a comb from her back pocket, combed her hair, and refastened the clasp holding it back. Her bangs lay flat, mashed by her helmet. She dampened her fingers and fluffed her bangs.

Of course! You always go to all this trouble for breakfast. Hee, hee, the voice persisted.

Trish stuffed the comb back in her pocket, wishing she could stuff the voice in the trash can along with the paper.

A man with the look of a reporter had joined her father for a cup of coffee. Hal introduced him as a writer for the *Blood Horse Journal*.

"How about if I get your breakfast, too?" Trish held out her hand for money. "Your usual?" At Hal's nod, she joined the line and waited to order. Trish studied the menu printed above the counter, in case there was something new she'd like to try.

"Told you I'd see you here," a voice said behind her.

She whirled around. Eric reached past her, picked up two trays and handed her one. "They make good hotcakes here. You need to pick up forks and stuff right there."

"I can handle it, thank you." Trish shook her head. Who did he think he was, telling her what to do? But his grin was easier to catch than a cold.

"My sister says I'm bossy."

"She's right." Trish tried to stop them but the words just leaped out.

"Y'all gonna order, or what?" The man behind the cafeteria-style counter settled back to wait.

Trish felt a blush creep up her neck. "Two orders. One egg over easy, bacon and hotcakes."

"Short stack or tall?"

"Huh?"

"You want two hotcakes or four?" His dark eyes laughed at her.

"Two. And put two eggs on the second order. Same way, over easy." She reached for a carton of milk and shoved her tray along the line. Why'd she feel like these two guys were ganging up on her? By the time she paid for the orders, the two plates of food appeared on top of the stainless steel counter. She loaded her tray and headed back to the table where her father was deep in conversation. He took the plate she passed him, nodded his thanks without breaking eye contact with the reporter.

"Don't mind Sam." Eric set his tray down beside Trish's. "He likes to give pretty girls a bad time. Once you get to know him, you'll like him." He pulled out the chair and sat down. "Actually, he likes to give everybody a bad time."

Trish looked at him, astonished. When she opened her mouth, no words came out. She watched as he attacked the scrambled eggs and dry toast. Who'd he think he was—her big brother? She already had one of those, thanks.

Trish spread butter and syrup on her hotcakes and seasoned her egg. She bowed her head for grace, and when she looked up again she could feel Eric staring at her.

"That takes a lot of nerve," he said softly.

"What?"

"Grace in public. That's just one more reason why I think I like you." He winked at her over the edge of his milk carton, then drank it half down.

Trish felt her mouth open—then close. Butterflies fluttered in her middle. As she ate her meal, she tried to listen both to her father's conversation and answer Eric's comments. Finally she gave up on her dad and enjoyed listening to Eric tell her about the people in the room. Famous trainers, world-class jockeys, renowned media, all were there and all were talking horses. She wished she could be a little mouse at each table, but then her mother had tried to teach her not to eavesdrop.

When she pushed her plate away, Eric stacked it on top of his, loaded the trays and returned them to the proper place.

"Tomorrow it's your turn," he announced as he sat down again, a cup of coffee in hand. "You want some?"

"No, thanks. And what makes you think we're—I mean, I'm—"

"Having breakfast together?" He took a sip of coffee. He shrugged. "We just are. You coming to the races this afternoon?"

"I—uh—I don't know." She turned to her father. He'd just finished his interview with the writer and heard the question.

He extended his hand. "Hi Red, I've heard a lot about you." He answered the question on Trish's face before she could ask it. "This is Red Holleran, leading apprentice jockey in the country."

Trish felt even more like someone who forgot to come in out of the rain.

"And about the races, I think not today. We've got to

get licensed, and then I'd better rest awhile. Trish, you could stay if you'd like."

Trish shook her head. She could see the tiredness around her father's eyes. That coughing fit in the barn hadn't helped any and yesterday had been a rough day.

"Then how about dinner?" Eric looked right at Trish. "I could meet you back at the barn after the program is done for the day."

Was he asking her for a date? Trish looked to her father, not sure if she even wanted to ask permission.

"Maybe another time." Hal pushed his chair back. "After you get to know each other a bit more."

Trish breathed a sigh of—relief—disappointment? She wasn't sure which.

CHAPTER 11

Hal slept all afternoon.

Trish slathered on sunscreen and lay out by the pool. *It would have been fun to watch Red race,* she thought. *And dinner? He probably meant hamburgers. But maybe not. Maybe it would have been a real date.* After a couple of hours of turning and toasting, she pushed herself to her feet. The spots she saw before her eyes reminded her of the last concussion, but they left as soon as she moved around some.

After changing clothes, she ambled out the door to the shopping center that surrounded the hotel. She spent an hour in the card shop, chuckling to herself as she chose cards to send home. But it wasn't as much fun without someone to show them to.

A T-shirt caught her eye in the next store, but she didn't have enough money along. There'd been no time to go to the bank before she left home. She'd have to ask her dad for some money.

By the time she bought a Diet Coke from the hotel pop machine and reentered the room, it was time to leave for the track for evening chores. She shook Hal awake.

"Dad? It's time to go feed Spitfire." She noticed the lines that had deepened around his mouth. "Dad?"

Hal groaned and blinked his eyes. "I didn't plan on sleeping the day away."

"Guess you needed it. I can go by myself if you want."

"No. You're not a legal driver for the rental car yet," he reminded her as he swung his feet to the floor. "We'll stop by the airport on the way back and get your name on that contract. Just in case you need to run an errand or something." He reached for her soda can and glugged a couple of swallows. "Now, that tastes good."

He seemed more himself on the drive back to the track. Spitfire welcomed them with nickers and head tosses. "You walk him around a bit," Hal said as he sat down in a lawn chair. "I've got some paper work to do."

By the time Trish and Spitfire returned, a couple of men had pulled up chairs and were visiting with Hal. Trish could hear them talking horses as she passed.

"Trish," her father called to her. "There's someone here I'd like you to meet."

Trish turned and walked back to the tack room.

"Patrick O'Hern, this is my daughter Trish." Hal put his hand on her arm. "I can remember reading about this man years ago, Trish. He retired from a good career as a jockey and went on to become a renowned trainer."

Trish shook hands with a rounded man no taller than she. His blue eyes twinkled above Santa Claus cheeks as he removed a battered fedora hat to greet her.

"So you be the lass they're all hummin' about." His brogue surprised Trish. "I'm pleased to meet you."

"Do you have a horse here?" Trish asked. From the abrupt silence she knew she'd said the wrong thing.

"Nay, lass, that was years ago."

Trish flashed a questioning look at her father. At the slight shake of his head, she nodded at the old trainer.

"It was nice meeting you, I've gotta go feed a hungry horse." As she left, she could hear the conversation pick up again. *Now what was that all about?* she wondered. Putting her curiosity aside, she went about the evening chores.

"Now you sleep well," she told Spitfire after forking out some dirty straw. She filled his water bucket and measured the grain, then leaned against his shoulder, stroking his neck while he ate. "It's strange not to be so busy that I don't know if I'm coming or going. Wish Rhonda were here, or Brad or David."

Trish really wished for help in the morning when she had to feed, ride, clean the stall, cool out the horse and tape his legs again. The early morning breeze touched her face with cool, velvet fingers, but by mid-morning the air felt heavy. Sweat ran down her back and neck.

"I'm sorry I can't help you more," Hal apologized. "I didn't plan for things to happen like this."

"I know. Don't worry about it. I needed some good old manual labor anyway." She rubbed her shoulder. "Now let's eat. I'm starved."

Trish had just finished saying grace when she felt a person take the seat next to her. She brushed a strand of hair back as she glanced sideways.

"Hi, sorry I wasn't there to help you this morning." Red grinned his irresistible grin.

Trish felt a tingle down to her toes. "Hi, yourself. I managed quite well, thank you." She laid her napkin in her lap. "How did you do yesterday?"

"One win, a show, one fourth, and we won't discuss the other." He took a bite of his scrambled eggs. "Is your dad feeling better?"

"How'd you know . . ."

"I read, remember. Besides, one look at him yesterday and I could tell he was having a hard time breathing."

"Yes, I . . ." Trish turned in her chair so she could really look at the jockey next to her. *I'd like to tell you what I'm worried about. No, I refuse to use the "w" word. It's about what's happening with my dad. I need a friend here.* "He needs a lot of rest and has to stay out of the dust."

"That's tough, the dust I mean. Well, the resting too."

"He didn't think it would be this hard, or we probably wouldn't have come." Trish kept her voice low so her father, who was talking with someone else, wouldn't hear her.

"Glad you told me. Does he need you with him all the time?"

"No. Not really, why?"

"I can help you some in the mornings, and maybe we can, I mean, I can show you some of the country when I'm not riding. Have you seen everything here at the track yet?"

"No. I—we—uhhh . . ."

"How about I show you and your dad around after we finish eating?"

"That'll be fine," Hal said when Trish asked. "We need to stop by the race office first and get our licenses. Are you riding today?"

"Not till late, so I won't have to be up in the jockey room so early." Red finished his milk in a long swallow. He raised an eyebrow at the question on Trish's face. "We have to report in two hours before our first race and return to the jockey room between races until we're finished for the day. Derby Day you'll have to check in about 9:30."

"But why?"

"Track rules. Don't worry, I'll introduce you to Frances Brown. She runs the women's room. You'll like her."

Trish felt a sinking in her stomach. She wouldn't be able to help get Spitfire ready. Good thing David would be here by then.

The Evanstons filled out the paperwork and paid their fees. Trish flinched at the cost of final entry. They were now officially listed as Derby contenders.

Eric proved to be a knowledgeable guide as they walked slowly around the track and through the tunnel under the grandstand. They saw the empty saddling stalls and walking paddock, fenced but open to viewers, as well as the owner's and trainer's lounge with a large screen for watching the races. They took the escalator to the jockey rooms.

"Wait here," Red told Trish at the entrance doors. "I'll call Frances."

A few moments later, an attractive woman with white hair smoothed back and tied at her neck, introduced herself. "I'm Frances Brown, kind of the room mother here. Mr. Evanston . . ."

"Hal."

Her smile felt warm and welcoming. "Hal, you go through those doors and Red will give you the tour. We'll meet you back at the coffee shop. Trish, the scales are through those double doors too. You need to let them know when you're going in so everyone's decent."

Trish couldn't believe her eyes as Frances showed her around. The men's jockey room at Portland wasn't as nice as this. Lockers, showers, a room with beds in case someone was tired, a whirlpool for injuries, sauna; and then they walked through a short hall to the recreation room with a snack bar for men and women. Some guys were already shooting pool and a TV flickered in one corner. The track monitor was showing videos of past Derby races.

Hal and Trish looked at each other and shook their heads. Things sure were different in Kentucky.

"Y'all come on up and visit and I'll introduce you to the other women jockeys around here," Frances invited. "We get into some pretty good story swappin' up here."

"I'd like that," Trish replied.

"You shown them the museum yet?"

"Nope, that's next," Red answered. "We'll meet you back outside, Trish."

"Thanks, Frances," Trish said as they turned the corner back into the women's room. "I'll probably see you next week."

"Any questions, you just ask," Frances said. "I'm here, seems like all the time."

The museum was located just outside the main gate. Trish realized immediately it would take hours to go through it. She glanced in the gift store just enough to know she'd like to spend more time there.

"Wait till you see the show in here on Thursday morning when they draw post positions." Red waved to a two-story oval room with other wings branching off. "This is the best museum on thoroughbred racing anywhere. Y'all oughta take the tour if you can. There's a library here and you can watch all the previous races that were filmed on video."

Trish stood in the center of the room and slowly turned around. Pictures, statues, displays, lists of all the Derby winners, all about the sport and industry she loved. She felt as if she were in the midst of greatness.

"Wow!" She closed her eyes to picture Spitfire's name on the list of Derby champions. When she opened them again, she saw Eric watching her. His grin surely matched her own. She could feel her cheeks stretching.

"That horseshoe out there is used only for the Derby," Red told them as they left the dimness of the tunnel under the grandstand. He showed them another place to their left, also banked with flowers but not nearly so grand. "The rest of the time this is for the winners. That seating area right up above it is for owners and their wives; we'll watch from there when we go to the races."

"Hey, Red," another jockey called. "If you're up on the first, you better get up there."

"See y'all later." Red smiled from Trish to her father. "Your badges will get you in anywhere." He walked backward as he talked. "Enjoy the races."

"Nice guy," Hal said as they followed the fence line to the backside.

"Yeah."

Even if he is bossy, her little voice chuckled.

Sunday morning two bales of straw were stacked by stall five when they arrived. Eric had the stall half mucked out when Trish returned from walking Spitfire.

"Gotta run." He grabbed up his helmet as he left.

That afternoon Hal felt much better, so he and Trish drove to Lexington to see the bluegrass country.

"People around here sure must love to mow." Trish had mild whiplash from trying to see both sides of the manicured highway at once. "See, even the pastures look like front lawns."

"Better'n our yard," Hal agreed with her.

"And the fences. I thought they'd all be white, but

some are black. And look at those barns."

"Even the barns are fancier than our house." Hal pointed out a particularly impressive structure on the top of a rise.

Trish rolled her window down. "It even smells good. I never believed what they said about the grass being blue, but it is." She pointed to a field that hadn't been mowed. The breeze rippled waves of deep blue-green across the stand of grass.

Hal pulled off the main highway so they could drive slower. He stopped at one field where a group of mares and foals grazed peacefully. "Aren't they something?" One youngster kicked up his heels and soon three raced across the rolling pasture. "Already in training for the races."

"So many at once." Trish rested her chin on her hands on the window. "I've never seen so many foals at one time."

"And look at the field of babies, all those yearlings." Hal pulled the car forward to the next pasture.

"Seems funny to call them babies."

"I know." Hal checked his watch. "We better head back. We'll try to come back tomorrow or Tuesday and visit the Horse Park."

"Maybe Mom and David'll want to see that, too."

"If they get here in time."

By the time they'd finished chores, Red hadn't made an appearance. Trish refused to admit she felt disappointed. After all, he hadn't said *when* he'd see her again. She decided to call Rhonda when they got back to the hotel, and tell her about the Jacuzzi. She slumped in her seat. Much as she loved being with her father, she did miss the rest of the three musketeers.

"You better cut it off," Hal tapped his watch later that evening. "Half-an-hour on long distance is enough."

"Okay," Trish sighed. "Dad says I gotta go. No, I'm not taking a picture of Eric. Rhonda, knock it off. He's just being nice to a stranger. Tell Brad all that's been going on. Bye."

She slumped against her pillows. There was a three-hour time difference. Right now Washington seemed terribly far away. She moped into the bathroom and started the water running in the tub. A hot soak would feel mighty good, and while it was filling she could talk to David and her mother. Her father had dialed home as soon as she'd hung up.

Sadness pulled Trish down into a puddle of lament after the call home.

Marge still wouldn't say for sure she was coming.

CHAPTER 12

Monday's paper carried a story about Trish and Spitfire.

"Can't these guys get anything straight?" Trish folded the paper and handed it back to her dad. They were sitting in their tack room about ready to go for breakfast.

"What don't you like?"

"I don't know, just a feeling I guess. Like they think I don't ride anything but Spitfire. That anything else I ride is just accidental. You know I've been doing all right at The Meadows."

"You and I both know you're an exceptional rider, but the rest of the racing world won't think so until you ride other horses at other tracks. That's just the facts." Hal shrugged his shoulders. "Let's go eat."

Eric didn't join them at the Track Kitchen like he usually had.

Trish caught herself looking around for him. The two bales of straw had been by their stall, so she knew he was at the track.

Oh, so you're missing him, are you? her little nagger snickered. *Thought you said he was bossy.*

Trish wiped her mouth with her napkin. Eric was just a friend, that's all. *And I need a friend here. Everyone else is so far away.* She picked up her father's tray and returned it with hers to the washing window.

"You want to go to the Horse Park today?" Hal asked as they drove out the gate.

Trish looked out her window. Heavy dark clouds covered the western sky. A brisk wind tossed trash in the air and whipped the branches of the huge shade trees around.

"I don't know. The weather doesn't look too good."

By the time they looped up onto the freeway, lightning forked against the black clouds. A few seconds later, thunder crashed louder than the sound of the car engine.

"Dad, let's go back to the track. You know Spitfire doesn't like loud noises."

"And he's never been through a midwest thunderstorm."

"Neither have I."

Jumbo raindrops pelted their car by the time they returned to the track. Lightning had just split the sky when Trish bailed out of the car by barn 41. She heard Spitfire scream as the thunder rolled over them, rattling the metal roof like a giant kettle drum.

Trish unhooked the web gate and slipped into the stall just as Spitfire reared, slashing the air with his hooves. She felt the wind of it on her cheek.

"Easy now, come on, Spitfire. We're here." She grabbed for his halter, all the while murmuring his name and comforting words.

Eyes rolling white, nostrils flared red, Spitfire trembled under her calming hands. The rain pounding on the roof above them drowned out her voice to any but the horse's ears. But that's who the sing-song was for.

"Here, Trish." Hal handed her a lead shank. "Run the chain through his mouth in case you need some control."

Trish did as she was told, and finished just as lightning turned the stable area blue-white. Spitfire threw up his head, but Trish clamped one hand over his nose and clutched the strap tight against his jaw with the other. She hunched her shoulders, waiting for the coming boom.

The crack sounded right overhead. Spitfire's front feet left the ground, but Trish stayed right with him. "Easy, boy, come on now. Nothing's gonna hurt you." He quivered as she stroked his ears and neck. Sweat darkened his hide.

"The storm's heading east, so maybe this won't last much longer." Hal stood on the opposite side of the colt, copying Trish's calming actions.

"Hope so. You sure this building's safe?"

"Lightning goes for the high points. The two spires on top of the grandstand would attract it away from here."

Trish sniffed. "What's that funny smell?"

"Ozone. From the lightning. That last one was right above us."

"Thanks."

Spitfire snorted like he was relieved, too. When the thunder rolled again, it was far enough away that he only flinched. The rain changed instruments from kettle drum to keyboard, singing off the eaves and thrumming on the gravel.

Trish took a deep breath. She wasn't sure if her hand shook of itself or because it strangled the colt's halter. She unclamped her fist and flexed her fingers.

Spitfire draped his head over her shoulder, shaken by an occasional quiver, just as a person shuddering after a crying spell.

Hal handed Trish a brush, and started on the other

side with another one. "Let's get him dried off."

"You okay here?" one of the track assistants asked.

"Now we are." Hal left off brushing and stood at the door.

"Yours wasn't the only horse shook up."

"Yeah, we don't get thunder and lightning much at all at home, and never like that."

"You need anything, you let us know." The man moved off.

Now that Spitfire was calmed down, Trish realized she was soaked. She hadn't been able to run between the drops during that downpour. She looked up from her brushing in time to see her dad shiver from the breeze that whipped down the aisle. He'd gotten wet, too.

"How about we go back to the hotel and get into some dry clothes?" She finished the brushing and gave Spitfire a last pat. "Come on, Dad." Shivers attacked her too as soon as she left the warmth of the stall. "Turn the heater on." She flicked the knobs herself as soon as she got into the car.

The heat pouring out the vents didn't make Hal quit shivering. Trish bit her lip as she heard his teeth chatter on a bad shake. "You want me to drive?" she asked.

"No. I'll hit the shower as soon as we get to the hotel, and you can make some coffee. Hot liquid inside and out oughta do it."

Trish turned the shower on as soon as she entered their suite so the bathroom could steam up. She filled the automatic coffeepot, and when it quit gurgling brought a cup to her father, who was still in the shower.

"Your coffee's here on the counter."

"Thanks, Tee."

Trish noticed the message light winking on the

phone. When she dialed the desk, they told her there was a package downstairs for her. By the time she got back up, the shower was quiet.

"Dad?"

"In bed. How about bringing me another cup of coffee?"

Trish poured a cup and carried it in to him. "My stuff came." She plopped the package down on his bed. "Think I'll study for a while since the sun's hiding. You gonna sleep?"

"Ummm. Can't believe how cold I got. I forget that my internal thermometer doesn't work the way it used to, thanks to the chemotherapy."

"Want something to eat or anything?"

"No, thanks." He handed her the cup. "Oh, maybe you better hand me those antibiotic pills in the amber bottle. Between the dust and the rain, I better be safe than sorry."

Trish wrote a paper for English, read two chapters in her history book, and took a nap. Her father was still sleeping when she got up, so she left him a note and drove back to the track to feed Spitfire.

"Where's your daddy?" asked the man at the gate. "He all right?"

"I hope so," Trish answered.

Spitfire was glad to see her, but it sure was lonely without her father.

The sound of his coughing greeted her when she opened the hotel room door. *Oh, God, what do I do now?* Trish thought of calling her mother, but what good would that do? She knew her father would just tell her to be patient; he'd feel better in the morning.

But he didn't.

Trish had set her alarm for six, and when she went to check on him, her father admitted to a temperature.

"Should we call a doctor?" Trish crossed her arms, hugging her elbows.

"No. Just give the antibiotics time to work. But I better stay in bed today. Trish, I can't tell you how terrible this makes me feel." The old, ugly rasp was back in his voice.

"No problem. I'll get someone to help me at the track. We can order room service for you."

"I don't feel much like eating. Maybe some orange juice and toast when you come back." He rubbed a hand across his eyes. "Are you sure you can handle things out there?"

"Da-ad. It's not like I haven't done all those chores before." She set two glasses of water on his nightstand. "Drink. I'll be back as soon as I can."

Trish hated to ask for help. Thoughts of how to take care of the horse and clean out the stall all at the same time nagged at her. She waved at the guard when she drove in and parked the car. Spitfire greeted her with his usual nicker. She poured his feed in the bucket and leaned against the colt's shoulder while he ate, trying to figure out what to do.

"How's your dad?" a familiar voice asked from the door.

Trish turned. One of her resident butterflies took a leap of pure joy. "Hi, Red. He's fi—how'd you know something was wrong?"

"Guard said your dad wasn't here last night or this morning. I knew he wouldn't leave you alone here unless something was really wrong."

Trish swallowed the lump that threatened her throat.

"He got wet in that rainstorm—chilled—and now he has a fever."

"So he's in bed?"

Trish nodded.

Eric appeared to be thinking hard. "Tell you what, I'll be right back." He dog-trotted up the aisle and out the barn.

Trish carried her saddle and bridle to the stall. Gallop was on the chart for Spitfire's work for the morning. She'd just have to take this one step at a time.

She was ready to mount when Eric reappeared—with help.

"Meet Romero and Juan."

Trish smiled at the two dark-haired young men.

"They'll clean out the stall while you ride. Then help you wash him down if you'd like. They're good with horses."

"Thank you." Trish nodded at each of them.

"Oh, they don't speak English," Red added.

"*Gracias*," Trish felt her tongue trip over the simple word. You'd think she'd never taken Beginning Spanish, let alone three years of it. But then, words like pitchfork and manure hadn't been part of the curriculum either. She headed for the tools stored in the tack box.

"I'll see you out on the track," Red said as he gave her a leg up. "Don't worry about these guys, they know what to do."

"Thanks." Trish stared down into eyes blue enough to drown in. She adjusted her helmet and nudged Spitfire forward. Her throat felt dry. She wasn't coming down with something—was she?

It was almost possible to forget her worries with the breeze fresh in her face and Spitfire tugging at the bit.

She kept him to a walk for half a circuit, then let him slow-gallop. He didn't fight her for more this morning, as if he knew she had enough to think about. Eric, mounted on a feisty gray, walked a circuit with her.

Later, she realized how much she enjoyed his teasing. Laughing felt good, but a clean stall and extra hands to help her wash the colt down and walk him out felt even better.

"You going for breakfast?" Eric showed up just as Trish had said her last *muchas gracias*.

"No. I need to get back to my dad. Thanks for finding me help." Trish opened her car door. "See ya."

Red leaned on the open door. "Where y'all staying?"

"The Louisville Inn. Why?"

"I'll call you later to see how things are going." He touched a finger to his helmet and trotted off.

Trish fixed a tray of food at the hotel buffet and carried it up to the suite. Her father was still asleep. She'd heard him coughing and wandering about several times during the night.

"Dad?" She moved things aside and set the tray on the nightstand. "I brought you breakfast."

"How's Spitfire?" Hal turned on his back and looked at her with real awareness for the first time since the chill. He cleared his throat.

Trish propped a couple of pillows behind his head and handed him a glass of orange juice. "He's fine, I'm fine, and you're looking better." She lifted the plastic dome off the plate and set the tray across his knees. "I'll go make some coffee."

She caught herself humming as she filled the pot. Amazing how her father's feeling better put a song in her heart.

"How are you handling everything?"

"Fine. Red brought me two stable hands and they cleaned out the stall while I worked Spitfire. Then I held him while they washed him down. I tried to talk some with them, but my Spanish is so slow they must think I'm an idiot."

Hal smiled around a bite of scrambled eggs. "I'm so proud of you, I can never begin to tell you how much. Thanks for the breakfast. Food tastes good this morning—finally."

Trish brought him a cup of coffee. "I'm going back to school Spitfire after the day's program starts. Since that's what you had on the schedule, I see no need to change it."

"Have you talked with your mother?"

"Not since Monday." Trish curled up in a chair and sipped her orange juice. "I'll call her tonight. You sound better, so we won't be lying."

"I'll take it easy today, but tomorrow I should be able to help. Tee, I've been thinking. Maybe we should hire Patrick O'Hern, that ex-trainer I introduced you to the other day. That would take some of the pressure off you."

"Why not wait and see? My two helpers are doing fine." Trish nibbled a piece of toast. "Not to change the subject, but Equinox is stabled right next to us. He's kind of high-strung."

"If we hired Patrick, he could become a permanent employee. We've been understaffed too long."

Trish looked at her father closely. He was serious about this. "We've gotten along okay up to now."

"I know." Hal handed her the tray. "I can't eat any more. I'll rest awhile, then get a shower. Can't believe how weak I am again."

"You were sick, running a fever, what'd you expect?"

"Yes, Dr. Evanston." A smile lifted a corner of his mouth. "How's your homework coming?"

"That's where I'm going now." She took the tray and placed it outside their door. Then, with books spread around her on the sofa, she attacked the list of assignments. That way she was able to blot out the idea of someone strange joining Runnin' On Farm.

When the phone rang, she about leaped out of her skin. What would she say to her mother? She picked it up before it could ring again. At the sound of Red's voice, she heaved a sigh of relief.

"Dad's sleeping again but feeling some better. Got him to eat a little."

"Is there anything I can do for you?"

Trish felt a warm glow in her heart. It was nice to know that someone cared. "No, but thanks. I'll be back later for schooling. Good luck on your mounts today."

She hung up the phone and stared at the framed print of the great horse Secretariat on the wall. The horse seemed to be looking right at her. It was a friendly look.

"You want some lunch before I go back?" she asked several hours later. Besides her homework, she'd written cards to Rhonda, Brad, her mom, and David.

Hal had taken a shower and was almost sleeping again. "No, thanks."

"How about if I call room service and they bring you a tray in about an hour?"

"Okay. But maybe you should put off the schooling."

"We'll be fine. Oh, and Spitfire needs new shoes, or the ones he has reset. One's loose."

"How about Friday?"

"Sure." Trish dialed room service and ordered soup

and more juice for her father.

Back at the track, the second race was being run. She and Spitfire just hung out for a while. She sat cross-legged in the corner of his stall, stroking his nose and scratching his ears. He nibbled on her fingers and blew in her bangs. She heard a whinny from the stalls behind them.

"Sounds like someone else has arrived." Spitfire raised his head and answered with a nicker of his own. "Sure, sure, tell him how good you are." She tickled the whiskers on his upper lip.

Schooling went as smooth as a well-rehearsed play. Spitfire followed his lines perfectly as they trailed behind the horses heading to the paddock for the fourth race. She stood him in the stall for a while, then walked around the paddock, pointing out the Chrysler Triple Crown emblem on a white wall and all the bright flowers. Spitfire seemed to understand every word.

"Look at that black," someone in the crowd commented.

"Which race is he in?"

Trish wanted to tell them but kept walking Spitfire.

Red waved to her before the trainer boosted him into the saddle. "How's it going?"

"Fine. Good luck." Spitfire played with the chain on his lead-strap when the mounted horses left the paddock to meet the ponies lined up just outside the tunnel. Another parade to post had begun. The crowd flowed back to find their seats.

———

"Hi, Mom." Trish caught the phone on the first ring again that night. Hal had eaten dinner and dozed off.

Trish and her mother talked about what was happening at home and the track before Trish asked Hal to pick up the extension. "See ya, Mom. Next week, right? Here's Dad." She hung up before she could hear her mother pause—or decline.

"Your grandparents are coming here for the Derby," Hal told her when she went in to kiss him good-night. "They'll be here next Friday."

"Good. What about Mom?"

Hal just shrugged his shoulders.

A nightmare attacked Trish again that night. This time it was a replay of the family reliving the accident at Portland Meadows. In the dream her mother cried—forever. Trish licked her dry lips and forced her eyes open. Another race was coming up—a big one. Was she ready for it? How would she control the butterflies that already flitted when she thought ahead?

She hated to close her eyes again.

Remember the name of Jesus? Her little voice was being helpful this time. What a nice change.

Trish closed her eyes and let the name of Jesus in big letters scroll across her mind. There He sat, smiling at all the children. She could never resist smiling back. And going right to sleep.

———

She'd just walked Spitfire back from another schooling session the next afternoon when a voice yelled to her. "Hey, Trish! Ya got company!"

CHAPTER 13

"Mom, you came!" Trish flew down the aisle and threw herself into her mother's arms. "And David." She strangled him with a hug next. "You guys are really here!"

"Why didn't you tell me earlier your father was sick?" Marge whispered into her daughter's ear as she hugged Trish again.

"He wouldn't let me."

Marge sighed. "I figured as much. How bad is he?"

"Better." Trish turned to her brother. "Some track, isn't it, Davey boy. Wait'll you see the rest. I can show you around after I feed the kid here."

Spitfire nickered when he saw David. "Hey, old man. You remember me, huh?" Spitfire bopped David's Seattle Mariner's baseball hat onto the dirt aisle. David picked it up and dusted off the brim. "Sure does. He act this way with anyone else, or does he save it all for me?"

Trish laughed at the sneaky expression on Spitfire's face. "He loves you, that's all." She showed David where they kept everything and measured out the evening feed.

"Hi, Trish, need some help?" Red stuck his head in the door.

"No, thanks. Hey, meet my family. They just got here.

Mom, David, this is Eric Holloran, better known as Red. He's a jockey here."

"Pleased to meet y'all." Red shook hands.

"How'd you do?" Trish asked.

"One win, a place, and a fourth. My checkbook is singing for joy. You still need the boys in the morning?"

"No, David here needs to work his muscles. And I'm glad you did well."

"Gotta run. Nice to meet y'all." He hesitated. "Can I buy you a Coke or something?"

"Thanks, but we're heading for the hotel as soon as we finish chores. Dad doesn't know they're here yet."

"Okay. See ya."

David looked from the retreating jockey to Trish. "Is there something going on here I should know about?"

Trish felt a blush creep up her neck. "David!"

Marge leaned against the half-wall, smiling at her daughter. "He seems like a very nice young man."

David snorted. He dumped the feed in Spitfire's box. "Let's go see Dad."

"You guys wait out here," Trish said as she dug in her pocket for the hotel key. "Dad needs a good surprise." She opened the door to the dark suite. "Dad?" She flicked on the light switch by the door.

"In here." Hal's voice sounded as if he just woke up.

"There's someone here who needs to talk with you."

"Okay, just a minute."

Trish clapped a hand over her mouth to stifle the giggles that bubbled up like a shaken soda can. She glanced at David to see the same look on his face. Marge had her tongue stuck in her cheek.

Hal wore his robe over a pair of jeans and was brushing his hair back with his hands as he came around the corner. The look on his face made the secrecy well worth-while. He hugged Marge first, and with her tucked against his side, he wrapped his other arm around his son's neck and squeezed hard.

Trish could also tell from her dad's look that he was thinking, "Thank you, God," just like she was. Her mother had come, fear or not. They were together, the way they should be. Trish felt a weight float away from her shoulders that she hadn't realized was so heavy.

They ordered room service, and sat around catching up for the next couple of hours.

"Good news," Marge said at one point. "Grandpa and Grandma are coming for sure; said they wouldn't miss it. They'll arrive on Friday."

"Will they stay long enough to go sightseeing with us?" Trish asked.

Marge shrugged. "Got me. You know what a rush they're always in to get back to their volunteering. I think they're busier now than when they were working."

Trish fell asleep that night with a smile on her face. Her family was all together.

"This area doesn't look at all like I expected," David said as he and Trish drove to the track the next morning.

"I know. The bluegrass country is really around Lexington. But wait till you see the Ohio River. It's huge. We haven't been anywhere yet since Dad got sick. Maybe this weekend." She parked by their barn. "We need to get you a badge later."

If it weren't for the difference in scenery, Trish would have felt as if she were home. She and David worked together like the team they'd become since their father's illness began. Having her brother there made her even more aware how much she'd missed him.

"Slow gallop now," David reminded her as he gave her a leg up. Spitfire stood quietly. "Is he feeling all right?" David nodded at the horse.

"Sure, why?"

"Well, he—he's quieter. Not such a clown."

Trish leaned forward and smoothed Spitfire's mane to one side. "I don't know. He seems to realize this is serious business. But you missed out on a real tantrum with the thunderstorm. Like at the airport. He *doesn't* like loud noises."

It had rained during the night and the morning air smelled fresh-washed and rose-petal soft on Trish's skin. She walked the colt once around the track, staying close by the outside rail. The rising sunlight sparkled on the twin spires above the grandstand.

At the second round, they broke into a slow gallop. Spitfire settled into the rocking gait, ears pricked, always aware of the horses working around him but not concerned. Trish relaxed along with him. There was no place on earth she'd rather be.

Red saluted her with his whip as he galloped by.

Trish pointed out the sights on the backside as she and David jogged over to the Track Kitchen for breakfast. On the way back they stopped at the office for his badge.

At ten the farrier arrived with his tools to shoe the colt. Spitfire stood like a perfect gentleman, only rubbing his forehead on Trish's chest as she held him.

Saturday morning after the chores were done, Hal called Trish and David into the office. "I think it's time we brought in someone else to help us," he said. "Now I don't want you to think it's because you haven't been doing a good job. You know better than that." He smoothed back a lock of hair that fell over Trish's cheek.

"I just think we need to make life easier for all of us, and thanks to Spitfire's win at Santa Anita, we can afford it."

"You have someone in mind?" David asked.

Hal nodded. "His name is Patrick O'Hern. Trish met him earlier this week. He had a tremendous reputation until . . ."

"Until—" David interrupted a long pause.

"Well, he—ummm—"

Warning bells went off in Trish's mind. Her father was on his helping-others-mode again. What had Patrick done?

"He became an alcoholic after his wife died and his whole life fell apart." Hal said the words in a rush, as if he couldn't wait to get them out. "But with God's help, he's turned his life around. I feel privileged to work with him. The man knows more about horses and racing than—"

"It's okay, Dad." David nodded and shrugged at the same time. "We trust you. If you think Patrick is who we need, that's great. Right, Trish?"

Trish nodded. "Sure. I liked him." But a squirmy little doubt dug in at the back of her mind.

"It's settled then. I'll page him and see if he can meet us up at the Track Kitchen."

The meeting with Patrick went according to Hal's plan. The man would start work on Monday.

The pace stepped up after the weekend. It seemed there were more reporters each day. Trish began to wonder where they all came from. All the Derby entries were now on site. As Trish watched the other horses work, she tried to compare them to Spitfire.

"You're just prejudiced," David said after one of her comments about the bad temper of the chestnut called

Going South. His trainer had posted a sign warning visitors to keep back.

"Where'd you ever get that idea?" Trish tried to look innocent, but the mischief dancing in her eyes gave her away.

They all fell easily into the new routine. Since Patrick stayed on the grounds, he fed Spitfire in the morning so Trish and David could sleep in a bit later. Then David mucked out the stall while Trish took Spitfire out on the track. The colt and Patrick hit it off from the first moment Patrick slipped the black a carrot chunk.

"Breeze him five furlongs," Hal said as Patrick boosted Trish up on Tuesday morning. "Trot once around to warm him up, then let him loose in front of the wooden stands." He pointed to the wooden bleachers constructed for owners and trainers by the gate to the track. "Patrick and I'll clock you from there."

Spitfire seemed to sense this morning was different. He played with the bit and danced sideways on the far turn. Trish snapped her goggles into place. As they came around the near turn, she angled him to the rail and let him extend to a gallop.

"Okay, fella, let's get ready," she crooned into his twitching ears. At the furlong marker she gave him his head and shouted, "Go, Spitfire." She crouched high over his withers as he exploded under her. With each stride he gained speed, like a sprinter off the mark. She remained in the high position, hands firm and encouraging. She almost missed the fifth marker, and the sixth passed before she could bring him down. They cantered on around the track.

The grin on her father's face told her all she needed to know. But her internal stopwatch already knew the colt had run well. The only question—could he last the mile and a quarter? Santa Anita had been a mile and an eighth. An eighth of a mile, one furlong, didn't seem far, unless you were running on pure heart by then. Races could be won or lost in the last stride.

"Here, lass, I'll walk 'im." Patrick reached for the lead shank.

"No, that's okay, I need something to keep busy. You guys are doing all the hard stuff." Trish relaxed after walking Spitfire out. His knee stayed cool to the touch, as if there had never been an injury. One more big relief.

Each day her internal aerial troupe took to practicing new routines. Anytime she thought of the coming race she could feel the butterflies leaping, fluttering, and diving.

"You okay?" Red asked her Wednesday morning at the kitchen.

"Why?"

" 'Cause y'all been stirrin' those eggs 'stead of eating them." He pointed to her plate.

"Guess I'm just not hungry."

"She always like this?" Red asked David. The two had become good friends in a short time.

Now Trish had two big brothers bossing her around. Except that when her hand touched Red's, it didn't feel the same as when she brushed David's. *Think about that later!* she ordered, after her shoulder tingled from Red's casual touch.

Thursday morning arrived either too soon or not soon enough—Trish wasn't sure which. This was *the* day for choosing post positions. She woke up to a mist hovering just above the ground. At the track, horses seemed to float in and out, like phantoms in a ghostly dance.

Marge and Hal attended the breakfast for owners, but Trish, David, and Patrick stayed with Spitfire, finishing morning chores. They went through the routine without talking, grabbed a quick bite to eat, and headed for the museum. Red had advised them to get there early, since the place would be packed.

The statue of Secretariat with its blanket of roses had been moved, and a podium with microphones was set up in its place in the oval room of the museum. Stage lights made the area brighter than day. TV crews were setting up their cameras, with cables snaking across the carpet.

As the time drew nearer, the room filled with spectators, owners, trainers, officials; and reporters with tape recorders, camcorders, and clipboards. Everyone was handed a sheet of paper with the twelve horses running listed.

"Here." Hal handed each of them a gold baseball cap with "Spitfire" lettered in crimson. "I meant to give you these before you left this morning. How'd everything go?"

"Fine." Trish bent the brim and settled her cap in place. "How was the breakfast?" She grinned at her mother. Even Marge, dressed in her navy silk suit, wore the crimson and gold hat.

Just then the lights went out. A multi-projector slide show set to music and narration sprang to life on a continuous screen that circled the room just under the second-floor railing. Trish felt a lump in her throat as she watched the life of a thoroughbred from foaling to the Derby. She kept turning to watch the scenes unfold as heroes of past Derbies galloped across the screen. A field of red tulips around the entire screen brought an "oooh" from many spectators. Haunting strains of "My Old Kentucky Home" faded away as the screen flashed names of this year's contenders. Spitfire, Going South, Nancy's Request, Nomatterwhat, First Admiral. Trish had to turn to keep reading. Dun Rovin', Equinox, Waring Prince, Who Sez, Spanish Dancer, That's All, and Sea Urchin. One of those names would be added to the list of greats.

The lights came back on. Now all Trish could see was the broad back of the man standing in front of her. The ceremony began. A horse's name was called, a number drawn from a container. The race secretary then placed that number beside the horse's name on a board for all to see.

Trish watched the people around her mark their papers. She didn't even have a pencil. A group cheered when Spanish Dancer drew position one. Number twelve for Who Sez didn't thrill his owners. Spitfire's name was halfway down the list. What would his number be?

Trish's butterflies went berserk.

CHAPTER 14

"Spitfire, position six." The waiting was over.

Trish listened with only half-an-ear as the remaining numbers were called. Number six meant they'd be right in the middle of the field.

As soon as the last number was posted, a reporter shoved a microphone in front of her father. Hal smiled at the question.

"You're right, the weather could indeed be in our favor. When you come from the Pacific Northwest, your horse better not mind the rain. Our colt runs well on a wet track. And position six can be either an asset or a handicap, depending on how fast he breaks."

He turned to answer another question. "No, there's been no problem with his knee for the last couple of weeks. Running at Santa Anita caused only a mild inflammation, nothing to be concerned about."

Nothing to be concerned about! Trish caught herself before she made any noises. *She'd* been concerned, that's for sure. If the press only knew all that had gone on.

She'd just thought about leaving when a young woman asked her a question. "That fatal accident out in Portland, you were involved in it, weren't you?"

Trish thought fast. "Yes. But I wasn't hurt much, a mild concussion."

"Do you feel that affected your riding? How about if you get caught in the middle during the Derby?"

Trish took a deep breath. Should she tell them she lost two races after that and considered backing out of another? No, this wasn't the place for total honesty.

"How can it *not* affect you when a friend is killed? But you go on. You ride each race as it comes. And you do your best. Guess that's about all you can do. Spitfire and me—we'll do our best."

"Good answer," David whispered in her ear as the reporters left to talk to others.

Hal was answering a man with ABC lettered on his microphone. Marge had a smile pasted on her face. Trish could tell the glue was wearing thin and the smile might slip off. She signaled David and the two of them took their mother's arms. "Let's go look at the trophies."

They could identify the owners and trainers by the groups gathered around them. The crowd was thinning out now, and the television crews were dismantling the cameras and rolling up their cables.

"How was the breakfast?" Trish shifted her attention from the humongous silver bowl in the trophy case to her mother.

"Huge. Hundreds of people."

"How about the trainer's dinner?" David asked.

"The hotel was beautiful and the food great but . . ."

Trish and David waited for her to go on.

"But—well, we met some very nice people." She paused, thinking. "I guess things are just different back here."

Trish looked around the room. "I guess."

"Like back in there. It's a fashion show. We just don't do things that way at home."

Trish grinned. "That's why I like it better down at the barns. Horses are easier than people. Did you see that woman all in white?"

"If those rocks she wore were real—" David shook his head.

"And the broad-brimmed hat. Why y'all don't know how na-ahce it is to see ya he-ah." Trish copied the accent and the gestures perfectly.

"Trish." Marge strangled on the laugh and bit her lip to keep from choking.

"We better get outta here before you get us in trouble." David appeared to be suffering from the same choking problem as his mother. He took both their arms and walked them past the visitor's information desk and out the front doors. When they reached the sunshine, they looked at each other and let the laughter spill. Hal found them a bit later, still giggling.

"Okay, what's going on?"

Trish and her mother looked at each other and started in again. Finally Trish took a deep breath and forced herself to look at her father, her face serious. "Y'all just don't dress us ra-aght, Daddy de-ah."

"The woman in white?"

"Oh, you noticed." Marge slipped her arm through Hal's.

"How could I not?" Hal shook his head. "Let's go check on Spitfire."

More reporters and writers crowded around them when they arrived back at the stable. Trish was beginning to understand what famous people meant when they talked about living in a fish bowl. She was scratching Spitfire's cheek with his head draped over her shoulder in his favorite position when someone asked if they could take her picture. Spitfire flinched as the flash blinded his eyes.

It was a relief when they headed back to the hotel.

"That slide show was the neatest thing I've seen." Trish popped the top on her can of Diet Coke and drank deeply.

"It really was." Marge leaned back in a chair. She slipped off her shoes and flexed her toes. "I'd love to see it again."

"The schedule is posted for showings." Hal stretched his arms over his head. "There any coffee left?"

David poured a cup for himself and one for his dad. "What a mass of people. This whole week is just one big party."

"No, it's lots of parties. Speaking of which, we have another one to attend tonight. The Churchill Downs Derby party." Hal looked at Marge.

"Do we *have* to?"

"We don't *have* to do anything. I'm sure they won't miss us, since I've heard there are usually about 500 people at this one. Besides, according to our daughter here, I don't dress you right. For dinner at the famous Galt House, that is."

Trish scrunched her eyebrows at him. "You don't say it right either."

"By the way, Red was asking for you."

Trish felt the heat blossom on her neck. "Oh?"

"Said he'd see you at evening feed if not before." Hal had a knowing twinkle in his eye.

Trish felt the blush spread to her cheekbones.

"Seems like a right nice young man."

"Da-ad!" She held her Coke can to her cheek. This was crazy. She didn't *like* him—did she? Did he like her?

Her father certainly seemed to think so. She threw a decorator pillow at David to wipe the smirk off his face.

"Just think, less than forty-eight hours." David shook his head. "And it's Derby time."

"Thanks a bunch." Now her butterflies leaped into life. A swallow of soda sent them into a frenzy. "You guys are really a big help."

"You kids want to go to the parade?" Hal set his coffee cup on the table.

Trish thought a minute. All those people. "How can we? Spitfire needs to eat about that time. The parade is late afternoon. I'd rather go somewhere for dinner that has great food, just us."

And that's what they did. By the time they were stuffed with hush puppies and babyback ribs, Trish was ready for bed. Mornings came so early.

"You and that black colt, lass, you're some pair," Patrick said the next morning as Trish leaped to the ground. "You both seem to know what the other's thinking. That'll be hard to beat out there."

"That means a lot, coming from you," Trish said. It was the first real compliment Patrick had given her. "I sure hope you're right."

They'd just finished breakfast when Hal and Marge ushered the two newcomers into the Track Kitchen. Trish leaped from her seat and threw her arms first around her grandfather, then her grandmother. Her grandmother's familiar lavender perfume lingered in the air.

"Can you believe we're all really meeting in Kentucky? I'm so glad you came." She stepped back to give them the once-over. "You look great." While her grandfather seemed a bit more stooped in the shoulders, Trish

156

didn't see any sign that he had been sick. Actually the two of them looked more alike than ever.

"Hello, David." The slender woman with snow-white hair leaned over to kiss his cheek.

By the time Hal had introduced Patrick, Trish had brought a tray with coffee for everyone.

"Are any of them decaf?" her grandmother asked. "I really must be careful, you know."

"I remembered. Those two on the outside are for you two." Trish handed one to her grandfather. She caught her father's wink as she handed him a cup. Careful was the operative word. When she thought about it, Trish knew where her mother got the worries—from *her* mother.

When Patrick excused himself, Trish followed suit.

"We'll be down later," her father said.

That afternoon was the running of The Oaks. Trish leaned on the iron rail around their box and watched both the spectators and the race. Tomorrow she would be up in the jockey room—waiting.

A chestnut filly with two white socks won by a length. The jockey riding her, Jerry Jones, would be up on No-matterwhat the next afternoon. He was known to bring in winners.

"Firefly would have taken it," Trish said to no one in particular. "Sure wish we could have brought her."

"She'll have her chance." Hal tapped her on the shoulder with his program. "And so will you."

Trish wondered later what he meant by that. As she flipped to her other side—for the third time—in bed that night, she couldn't quit thinking about the coming race. What if someone fell? What if Spitfire got hurt? What if they lost? What if they won? The what-if's were driving her right out of her mind.

She tried to pray. The questions paraded across her mind instead. She recited her Bible verses. Ahhhh, she felt a little calmer. *Relax*, she ordered her muscles. They ignored her.

Maybe they should have gone to one of the parties they'd been invited to. Then she wouldn't have so much time to think. She turned over—again.

Finally Trish sat up in bed and turned on the light. The soft glow burnished the curve of the carved eagle wings. Trish smoothed a finger over the intricate carving. Her song ". . . raise you up on eagle's wings, bear you on the breath of God . . ." drifted through her restlessness.

What would it be like to catch the air currents and spiral higher and higher? To feel the wind in your wings? She sighed. She knew what it felt like to be held ". . . in the palm of His hand."

"Thank you, Father," she breathed. "Thank you."

The peace of sleep was shattered by screams and groans. By sirens and shock. By dirt and blood. The nightmare rocked through her with a vengeance.

Trish jerked upright, gasping for air. She'd felt as if someone were sitting on her chest. She propped her shoulders against the head of the bed and waited for her heart to stop pounding. It was just a nightmare. And nightmares were always worse than reality.

You're scared! her little nagger whispered. *You have the big race tomorrow—no—today, and you're scared to bits. Look at you shake. You shouldn't be afraid.*

Trish clapped her hands over her ears, but it didn't help. She *shouldn't* be scared. But then, who wouldn't be. The Kentucky Derby was a *big* deal. Half the world would be watching.

That thought didn't help at all. Instead, she got up

and went to the bathroom. She got a drink of water and climbed back into bed. This time she painted and repainted a picture of Jesus on her mental screen until she slipped off to sleep.

Her butterflies leaped into life with the buzz of the alarm. It would have been nice if they'd overslept.

As usual, Patrick had already fed the hungry black colt. He hummed a happy tune as he polished their racing saddle.

After greeting him, Trish whistled softly. Spitfire, his head already over the web gate, nickered his happiness at seeing her. He nuzzled her cheek and whiskered her hand, begging for his carrot treat. Trish didn't disappoint him.

The sky was overcast as Trish trotted him out onto the track half an hour later. The forecast was for possible thundershowers.

"And you don't like thunder, do you?" Trish carried on a conversation with his ears. They twitched backward and pricked forward again, keeping track of everything around them. Trish rose in her stirrups as they trotted around the track. When he settled to a slow jog, she sat down again and enjoyed the ride. A pounding trot hadn't helped her stomach any.

Her father was answering questions again when they returned to the stall. Patrick and David washed the colt down, getting their own steam bath in the process. Trish washed Spitfire's face with a soft sponge. He nibbled at the sponge, then shook his head, spraying her with water.

"Knock it off." She raised an arm to keep the drops out of her eyes. Spitfire curled his upper lip, as if he were laughing at her. They scraped him dry, blanketed him, and then Trish took the lead shank to walk him out. David had already cleaned the stall and spread new straw.

Trish missed her messed-up conversations with her two Spanish-speaking helpers. They'd called Spitfire *muy cabrillo,* beautiful horse.

"How you feelin'?" Red fell into step beside her.

"Scared. You just startled me."

"You were kinda off in dreamland."

"No, I wasn't." But Trish knew her mind had been somewhere else. That was dangerous. She needed to concentrate on Spitfire in case something spooked him.

"You going for breakfast?"

Trish shot him a pained look.

"Oh. Butterflies?"

"A belly full."

"You better eat something. I'll see you later up in the jockey's room. You play pool?"

Trish shook her head. How would she get through all those hours up in the jockey room?

"How about Ping-Pong then? We'll find something to make the time pass. See ya." He trotted off.

"Do you think he ever walks?" Spitfire shook his head.

Trish managed to get down a piece of toast. She bypassed the milk and drank apple juice instead.

"You'll be fine." Her father had his mind-reading skills in gear.

"Wish I could stay down at the barn with you guys. At least I'd have something to do there."

"I know this is different and difficult. But the day'll be gone before you know it."

Trish nodded, but this time she doubted her father was right.

Spitfire shone from all the brushing. His hooves gleamed, mane and tail waved, flowing free just as Trish liked. Neither she nor her father cared for the decorative braiding some stables used. The tack was soaped and polished.

It was quiet around the stalls. Once in a while a visitor dropped by, but horses and people were both getting a rest. Trish leaned back in the lawn chair. If only she could stay here.

"You want me to walk you over?" David asked.

Trish glanced at her watch. It was time. Why did she feel like she was being walked to the execution block?

Patrick clasped her cold hands in his warm ones. "Don't be worryin', lass. Just give it your best."

Trish nodded. She was afraid if she opened her mouth, the butterflies would strangle her.

In spite of the lowering sky, the infield was fast-filling with spectators. All the grandstand and bleacher area had been reserved weeks before, but crowds had poured into the infield since the gates opened at 8:00.

"Did you see the car?" David nudged her arm. They were almost at the tunnel.

"The red one?"

"Yeah. Just think, it'll be yours when you win. A red Chrysler Le Baron convertible."

"I can't think about that now." Trish chewed her lip. Her swallower was too dry to work.

David handed her her sports bag at the bottom of the stairs to the second-story jockey rooms. "See you in the saddling stalls."

Trish stepped on the escalator. She turned once and waved to David, who waited at the bottom.

Frances Brown was the only one in the women's

jockey room. She sat at her desk, reading a coffee-table-size book. "Hi, Trish. I brought this in for everyone to look at." She turned to the front cover. The title, *Kentucky Derby*, was lettered in white above a racing thoroughbred. "The pictures are fantastic. I've never seen a better book."

An hour later Trish was still reading it. The pictures were great but so was the text. She learned things about the history of the track and racing she'd never heard before.

Since the first race of the day was at 11:30, several other women came in. Trish was the only female riding in the Derby. She put the book down when she heard someone call her name.

"Trish, Red's in the other room asking for you." Frances smiled at her. "Glad you like my book."

"Where did you get it? I want one."

"At the museum gift store. You go eat something if you can. You'll feel better."

Trish wasn't so sure. At the roar of the crowd on the monitor, her butterflies thought the applause was for them. They added new routines to their show. Trish wrapped both arms around her middle. *Please God, help me.*

CHAPTER 15

It was raining.

Trish stood at the window looking out over the rooftops of the grandstand. The rain looked like sheets of gauze blowing in the wind. She'd watched race number two on the monitor. It had finished just before the rain veil hit.

She heard the click of pool balls from the table behind her.

"What's a five-letter word for dog?" asked a jockey who was working a crossword puzzle at one of the tables.

"Hound."

"Thanks."

Trish didn't turn around until Red handed her a Diet Coke. Then she leaned her hips against the windowsill and looked up at the monitor. Another previous race was running.

"I watch those all the time." Red gestured toward the screen. "Helps to understand each jockey's style."

"Where do you watch, here?"

"Over in the museum. It's a big screen too, so you can see more. Plus the track has a video library."

"Wish I could be down at the barn. At least there's something to do there."

"Pretty quiet yet. Spitfire's probably sleeping. With

the all-night partying on the streets around the area, the horses need some extra sleep, too."

"I suppose." She rotated her neck. "Usually I have at least a couple of mounts, more like three or four. That keeps me hustling. Or I help David on the backside."

"Trish." He paused. "How long you gonna be around after the race?"

She shrugged. "Depends on how we do. Dad just says wait till after the Derby, then he'll decide."

"But you're entered in all three races of the Triple Crown?"

She nodded. "Why?"

It was his turn to shrug. "I'd like to spend some time with you. Maybe a drive or a movie. Something."

"Oh." Trish took a long swallow of her Coke. She looked up to find those blue-blue eyes studying her. "I'll ask my dad."

"Good. See you later. Gotta get ready for my next ride." His grin made her feel good.

"Good luck."

Trish returned to the women's room to find Frances swapping tales with one of the jockeys. They broke off to watch the fourth race. Red brought his mount up on the outside, hanging back with another horse until the stretch.

"Now!" Trish joined in the hollering, cheering him on.

Red went to the whip and bore down on the leader. He won by a length. When the camera showed the winner, you could hardly recognize horse or rider for the mud. But Red's grin was contagious even over the television.

The rain had quit but the track was now officially

listed as muddy. From the looks of the last riders, muddy was an understatement.

Maybe the rain lulled them to sleep. Trish suddenly realized her stomach was butterfly-free. She sprayed furniture polish on her five pairs of goggles and wiped them off, stacking them together, ready to snap over her helmet. Then she buffed her boots. *When had the butterflies disappeared?* She didn't know, but didn't really care either. The peace she'd prayed for had crept right in. She felt good. It wouldn't be long now.

She was all stretched and ready when the call came.

"Give it all you've got," Frances told her. "It's about time we had a woman in that red horseshoe."

"Thanks." A couple of butterflies tried to break out, but Trish swallowed them down. On the scale, her total weight with saddle and lead registered 126 pounds, like every other Derby jockey. She followed the others down the stairs and through the lines of waving and shouting spectators to the paddock. It wasn't raining.

Trish breathed in deeply of the fresh-washed air and rotated her shoulders. Her parents and grandparents were dressed in their best. David and Patrick waited with Spitfire. The colt nickered when he saw Trish.

"You ready?" Hal asked.

At Trish's nod, David punched her lightly on the shoulder. "You can do it."

Trish kissed Spitfire on his nose. He wuffled in her ear as she hugged him. "This is it, fella. You ready to show them what we can do?"

"Riders up." The official call was clear.

Trish felt a lump grow in her throat when she looked into her father's eyes. "I love you," she whispered in his ear as she threw her arms around his neck and hugged him. She hugged her mother next. "Thanks for being here."

Marge nodded. Her sniff told of tears hovering.

Then Trish hugged her grandparents. "I can't tell you how glad I am you came."

"We wouldn't have missed it," her grandfather said.

Trish took a moment, looking deep into David's eyes. "I'm glad you're my brother. We couldn't have made it without you."

David gave her a quick hug, the kind that brothers give when they're more used to swats and jabs. "Just win for us."

Patrick touched her hand. "We'll all be praying, lass."

Hal gave her a leg up and squeezed her knee. "You know what to do. God bless."

Patrick led them out to join the line in position number six. There was no turning back now.

Trish's pony rider picked her up at the tunnel. The gray horse wore roses in his braided tail and mane. As Spitfire cleared the tunnel, Trish heard the bands playing and everyone singing "My Old Kentucky Home." She reached forward to pat her horse's black neck. Head high, ears forward, Spitfire waltzed to the music. The way he floated over the ground couldn't be described any other way. They turned and trotted back before the grandstand again. Trish saw lightning fork from the dark sky to the west. Thunder rumbled in the distance.

Equinox trotted in front of them, giving his handler a bad time. Sweat already darkened his shoulders.

As they cantered toward the backside, Trish could feel Spitfire relax even more. The only thing bothering her was the dense black cloud that blanketed the sky above the barns. If only it would hold off until after the race.

The wind picked up even as the parade of horses began entering the starting gate. Number one, Who Sez, refused to go in. Four green-jacketed gate men got behind and shoved the horse into the gate. The next four walked right in. Equinox reared when the lead was transferred from pony rider to handler. The jockey clung like the professional he was, but Trish knew he must feel shaky about it.

Spitfire danced to the side but obeyed when Trish ordered him forward. He stood quietly in the gate. Dun Rovin' on their right acted spooky, tossing his head and rocking back and forth.

"Watch him," his handler said from his place up on the side of the gate by the horse's head.

Trish kept her eyes straight ahead, focused on the spot between Spitfire's ears. He was balanced, ready.

As Spanish Dancer, number twelve, stepped into the gate, the entire area turned blue-white. Thunder crashed right on top of them. The gates sprang open.

Spitfire threw up his head. Off balance, he slipped at the bound from the gate. Equinox bumped hard against him.

Trish fought to hold his head up. Spitfire gained his footing, but by the time they were running true, the field had left them behind.

"Okay, fella, bad start, so now we gotta make up for it." Trish's steady voice cheered him on. They were two lengths off the pace as they passed the stands for the first time.

It looked like a wall of haunches ahead of them as the last four horses ran shoulder to shoulder. Trish waited patiently until one drifted to the outer rail and she had a hole to drive through. She took it without a flinch.

They came out of the clubhouse turn running neck and neck with number eight in the middle of the field. Trish eased Spitfire to the right until they ran on the outside.

Two lengths in front of them, the horse on the inside was bumped and crashed into the rail.

The jockey flying over the horse's head barely registered, it happened so fast. "Come on, fella," Trish crooned around the clench in her gut. Only three horses pounded on ahead of them. Trish could tell the going was slow, but Spitfire didn't mind.

She had pulled down three goggles already. The horse in front seemed to stop, he slowed so much. Spitfire was running easily in third. At the mile marker, Trish made her move.

"Okay, Spitfire, this is it." She crouched tight over his neck, feeling herself part of her colt—as if they were one body, one mind. And that mind was on the two horses leading.

Spitfire stretched out. He picked up the pace, running as if the track were dry and fast.

"Come on, Spitfire!" Trish hollered in his twitching ears.

The second-place horse fell back in a couple of strides. Only Nomatterwhat was left.

One furlong, an eighth of a mile, to go. Trish willed her black colt to give it all he had. She could see the white posts ahead.

"Now, boy, now!" They drew even.

Jones went to the whip. Neck and neck, they thundered toward the finish line.

Spitfire stretched his nose past the sorrel. Then his neck. His shoulders. He won by three-quarters of a length.

"Yowee!" Trish yelled at the top of her lungs. She straightened her legs, standing in the stirrups to slow Spitfire down. "You did it, you gorgeous hunk of horse-flesh, you did it!"

Tears streamed down her face, creating furrows in the mud.

"Thank you, Father, thank you. The Derby. We won the Derby!" She turned and cantered back to the finish line. Past the screaming and cheering crowd, past the cameras lining the inside rail, to that grassy horseshoe outlined in red tulips.

Trish stopped in the center of the track and turned Spitfire to face the crowds, to receive his applause, his just due. "You did it, fella, see how good it feels?" She raised a mud-crusted arm and waved. As her arm came down, she leaned forward and hugged her horse's neck. The applause thundered louder.

David and Patrick reached them first. David slapped her on the knee and pumped Trish's hand. "I didn't think you two would pull it off after a start like that."

"My old heart nearly stopped." Patrick patted his chest. "As I said, you two are really something."

"I told you he doesn't like thunder." Trish looked across the crowd for her father. He had Marge by the arm, helping her negotiate the rutted and muddy track. Behind them, two men in business suits assisted her grandparents. Trish could see Marge had been crying, in fact, still was. The radiant smile she lifted for her daughter said the tears were those of joy.

"All I can say is thank you, God," Hal said as he clenched Trish's hand.

"You're safe," Marge said around her tears.

"And we won." Trish swallowed hard.

"Come on." Hal grasped the reins and led them through the mob and into the horseshoe.

Spitfire stood, head high as the officials draped a blanket of red roses across his withers. Cameras clicked while a sheaf of roses was handed to Trish. More cameras flashed in the dimming light. Trish leaped lightly to the ground. She reached up and pulled Spitfire's head down for a quick scratch and a hug.

At that moment, Spitfire noticed David's hat. He flipped the brim with his nose and sent it flying.

David looked at Trish and shook his head. "Can't you teach this clown any manners?" People around them laughed and applauded again.

"Come on, old son," Patrick slipped a halter over Spitfire's head. "Let's get you to the testing barn." As he led the colt away, Trish and her parents were escorted up the white ramp of the horseshoe to stand behind the row of four silver trophies. The large fancy one was given each year to the winner, then returned to the museum with the winner's name engraved on it.

"This is unusual," the Master of Ceremonies announced. "This time all these trophies go to the same family. Owner and trainer, Hal Evanston. Jockey, his daughter, sixteen-year-old Tricia Evanston. This bunch keeps things in the family."

Trish, Hal, and Marge waved again. Trish couldn't look at her mother for she knew she'd cry in earnest then.

Hal stepped up to the microphone. "I can't begin to tell you how I feel. I thank all of you, and our Heavenly Father for making this day happen." He waved again. "And yes, we'll be going on to the Preakness, God willing."

Trish felt a leap of excitement. Could anything top this?

"And now, the first female jockey in history to win the Kentucky Derby, Tricia Evanston."

Trish cleared her throat. She looked across the sea of people filling the stands. Reporters with cameras and camcorders crowded the infield in front of her.

"Every jockey dreams of being up here one day. I don't think the feeling would be any different, whether you're a man or a woman. This is my dream come true, helping my father make *his* dream come true. Thank you."

"Stay right here," the Master of Ceremonies said, and he introduced the representative of the Chrysler Corporation.

"It is my great pleasure to present you, Tricia Evanston, with the keys to that Le Baron convertible over there." He placed them in her hand. "Is this your first car?"

Trish nodded. "Thank you," she stammered. She'd forgotten about the car. What would her mother say about this?

After answering more questions, shaking all the hands that reached for them, smiling for the cameras, and answering *more* questions, the security officers opened a pathway through the crowds and escorted the Evanston family across the track and into the tunnel.

"Way to go, Trish," a familiar voice called from the stands above her head. Trish looked up to wave at Red.

The escort took them upstairs to the director's office where more congratulations were extended. Trish wished David were able to be with them. Instead, he had joined Patrick and Spitfire back at the testing barn.

"Trish, I'm Bill Williams from *Sport's Illustrated.*"

Trish shook his hand. "I'm glad to meet you."

"Before you change, could we go out to the backside and get some more pictures of you and Spitfire? I'd like a headshot of the two of you for the cover of our next issue."

Trish looked around for her father. He was talking with someone across the room. "I—I guess." *The cover of Sport's Illustrated. What's Rhonda gonna say about this?* She almost giggled at the thought. *And what's Mom gonna say?*

What could she say?

"You better wash your face first," Marge whispered in Trish's ear. Trish excused herself and did just that.

They all trekked across to the backside to barn 41. Patrick had Spitfire all washed and dried, but quickly slipped the white bridle back in place. Spitfire draped his head over Trish's shoulder, as he loved to do, and pricked his ears when someone snapped their fingers behind the photographer's head.

"Thank you," Williams said. "And I can call you at the Inn for an interview time?"

Trish nodded. "That would be fine."

"We have another reception." Hal laid his hand on Trish's shoulder. "You better go change."

Marge reached to hug her daughter before she left. "I was so scared and so proud at the same time, I didn't know what to do but pray. I thank God for taking care of you, and for prayer. I couldn't have gotten through this otherwise."

"Mom, I'm so proud of you." Trish hugged her mother back. "No matter how afraid you were, you came through. You came and watched me race. Dad and I really needed you."

Hal wrapped his arms around both of them. "That's

right. We're in this together. And now it's on to Pimlico."

Spitfire shoved his head between them and blew in Trish's ear. He was ready too, for another carrot and more scratching.

ACKNOWLEDGMENTS

My thanks to Emergency Medical Technician Ted Bingham, who told me procedures for emergency vehicles. My favorite medical expert is Karen Chafin, whose nursing experience is invaluable when I need a quick medical question answered. She's also my sister—I'm blessed.

Several hours listening to jockey Patty (P.J.) Cooksey, trainer Glinny Dunlop Bartram, and jockey room mother Frances Brown swap horse stories in the women's jockey room at Churchill Downs was worth the entire trip to Kentucky, even if I hadn't been able to see the Derby. Thanks to all of you for enriching my stories by increasing my knowledge.

Linda Wood introduced us to Churchill Downs, the site and the people. Thanks for sharing your time and knowledge.

So many people answer so many questions for me. Thank you all.